CU00706864

Diamonds Fall

REBECCA M. GIBSON has always loved a good story. She wrote *Diamonds Fall* after a certain Miss Hoddington tumbled into her head, intruding upon a perfectly peaceful walk.

Rebecca lives and works in Devon, UK dreaming of a white manor and the woods where oceans of bluebells lie in wait.

Diamond's Fall

Rebecca M. Gibson

TANNER PRESS UK

This is a work of fiction. Names, characters, places and incidents either are a product of the author's imagination or are used fictiously. Any resemblance to actual persons, living or dead, events or locales is entirely coincidental.

Copyright 2015 © Rebecca M. Gibson

Published by Tanner Press
Tanner Press UK

Cover and interior design by Molly Phipps
All rights reserved

The moral right of the author has been asserted

No part of this publication is to be reproduced, transmitted or utilized in any form or by any means, electronic, mechanical, photocopying or otherwise, without the prior permission of the author.

ISBN: 978-0-9932963-0-7

To my mum, just because...

Chapter One

England, 30th May 1895

A whip cracked. The sound reverberated through the air like a gunshot. As the carriage jerked into action, a young woman stared out the window. Her reflection sat beside her like a ghostly twin. Together, they looked unknowing towards their impending future.

Once in the midst of a vast park the vehicle came to a stop and Annabel Hoddington stepped down. An awed silence fell over everything. The gowned and suited figures - perched on top of checked blankets - froze.

The Hoddington family was a magnificent example of high society. They symbolised everything the spectators dreamed of, a constant illusion of unachievable perfection. Seizing his chance, a journalist leaning against the fence began furiously scribbling in his waiting notepad.

The park itself seemed to hold its breath as Annabel took her first step. The figures remained rigid with excited expectation. There was a collective sigh as she began to walk away from them.

Annabel inhaled, filling her nose with the scent of fresh flowers and mown grass. Satisfaction coursed through her body as she felt every pair of eyes fixated on her slightest movement. She had been officially out in society for two years, yet it was tonight she would raise herself further above everyone else. Tonight was when her life would begin.

She strode past her admirers with a practiced air of indifference, a small smile tugging at her mouth. Her chaperone, some distant relation of her mothers, chattered incessantly. As she spoke she wielded her hands in front of her face, as if conducting an invisible orchestra. Annabel studiously ignored her, glancing around to make sure she was still being followed by every gaze present. She even took a turn between the upper and lower class border just to give those shabby, poor persons a glimpse of the splendour they would never achieve. She figured she was doing them a favour, placing a positive experience in their otherwise dull lives.

When her chaperone's chatter had turned to the topic of her uncomfortable shoes and overly tight corset, they decided to rest on a nearby bench. The plump girl gratefully threw herself down, prepared to stay there indefinitely. Hiking up her ruffled skirt somewhat she balanced her ankle upon her stocking clad knee. She groaned obscenely as she removed her shoes – she could only have been in them for twenty minutes at the most. Annabel looked away from the sight, repulsed and glad the spectators had returned their attentions to their picnics.

Rolling her pretty eyes, Annabel turned around. Gazing in front of her she realised she was looking towards a dense forest, a few hundred yards beyond the park's edge. Annabel had never been in the forest before.

She sat for several minutes, perched on the edge of the seat, watching as the leaves swayed in the gentle breeze. She wondered what it might be like to hear them rustle against each other, or to be surrounded by the scent of wild flowers. As she wondered, her cheeks heated up with an uncharacteristic, rebellious impulse to enter. After all, it was her birthday. Come tomorrow she would never leave the adoration of people's gaze. This was her only chance. Glancing around like a criminal, noticing that her chaperone's eyes were now closed, her head lolling to the side, Annabel stood carefully and crept out of sight.

She walked faster than usual, looking back every few yards to check - for the first time in her life - that she had not been noticed. It was naïve to think no one had seen her but Annabel was too self-absorbed to register the hiss of chatter building behind her. The forest was ever so slightly up hill, the ground uneven beneath her feet. Unused to exertion she entered the line of trees flushed and short of breath. Her feet crunched on stones and fallen leaves whilst the small heels of her boots sunk into the damp ea rth.

Annabel looked up. Her breath caught in a sigh at the sight before her. She had never seen anything more beautiful in her life.

She had gazed upon this very forest from her bedroom

window a million times. From a distance the dense gathering of trees had seemed rather magical. Once inside the magic doubled. The trees embraced each other lovingly above her head whilst the birds sang in their own melodic symphony.

An ocean of bluebells washed over her feet, filling her nostrils with sweet perfume as she strolled further into its depths. Every nerve ending in her body ignited, such as she'd never felt before. It was as if everything had ceased to exist, as if the world itself had stopped spinning.

Annabel found that for the first time in her life, she actually wanted to be alone. She noticed how the sun shone at the perfect angle through the thin leaves to catch the vivid purple of the flowers. She watched it dart off her embroidered skirt, casting rainbows in the air around her. The insects flying lazily above the plants looked, in this setting, like fairies gliding through their very own fairy tale.

Unseen, or so she thought, Annabel removed one of her gloves and crouched down to touch the tiny purple blooms on the floor, smiling still wider at the velvety feel of the petals against her fingers. The musky smell of fresh earth and fallen leaves, so far from the usual artificial smell of the manor, was oddly reassuring from down there. She straightened slowly, with a slight creak of her corset, to gaze up at the fluffy clouds through the trees and feel the rare caress of the sun's warm rays on her face. She untied her hat so she could feel the heat of the warm weather. Her hair glowed a celestial gold from the carefully erected structure atop her head.

A twig snapped.

Annabel whirled around thinking of journalists, accidentally dropping her lace glove to the floor. Her heart rate increased, her chest rising and falling quicker than usual. She scanned the line of closely packed trees, laughing quietly to herself when she noticed no-one was there. Fixing her gaze back to the bluebells beneath her feet, she bent to retrieve her glove, with the intention of getting back to the park as quickly as possible. She still had a big day ahead of her, she needed to return home.

Just as she located the expensive lace in the grass, her gaze admiring the effect for a few seconds, there was another noise to her right. She whirled around again, her ears prickling on high alert. Her legs were rooted to the floor as if they had been there as long as the trees themselves. A sheen of sweat beaded on her upper lip.

Another noise from a different direction.

"Who's there?" Annabel called in her most authoritative manner. "I can hear you, you cannot hide from me. My father-"

She was cut short in the middle of her threat as the footfalls seemed to come even closer. She scanned the closely packed trees frantically, her eyes roaming in her head, as she tried to catch sight of whatever retch had followed her. She hoped it wasn't someone poor. That would not do, especially not today.

Annabel's corset creaked once more as her breathing turned heavier, the constraints of her clothing unused to such deep breaths. She wasn't even sure why she was so frightened, she had been chased by the likes of journalists before. Perhaps it was the possibility of her being caught alone in an unsuitable area that scared her. The story would be all over the gossip columns, casting a shadow across her impending announcement. She sighed when she heard nothing more for several seconds. Turning to leave, she replaced the glove on her slender hand.

That's when she heard the heavy foot falls start back up again. They staggered directly behind her and before she could move so much as an inch, she felt a white hot pain shoot through her head. Her knees smacked into the sun dried ground, crashing against a concealed rock in the mud. Unconscious, her body crumpled to the floor.

When she came too, Annabel's head was spinning, her vision blurred. She was lying on her front, disorientated but becoming painfully aware of a strong smell of liquor. It was different to the sweet, almost comforting smell of it in the parlours of the manor. This scent was vile, mixed with the pungent smell of stale sweat. Before another second had gone by, a coarse hand clasped itself tightly over her mouth, shoving some rough, sour tasting material between her teeth in the process. Too late, she tried to scream.

The hand, feeling her attempt to seek help, dug it's over grown fingernails into her soft cheek. She made a muffled moan of pain as she fought for breath. Fear and rage clawed at her stomach like bile. She tried to struggle but her hands had been bound behind her back. Pain tore at her wrists as she moved. She tried to open her mouth - just wide enough to sink her teeth into the disgusting flesh - but it wasn't possible. She squirmed left and right as much as she could, kicking out her legs.

Annabel's movements felt sluggish with the pain still searing in her temple. It was now she registered the slow, sticky wetness of her own blood dripping down the side of her face. She was not used to being out of control and that scared her more than anything.

There was hot, fast breath on her neck. A full male form was pressed against her, in a way that made his intentions frighteningly clear. She kicked out with new fight but his breath seemed only to quicken at her struggle.

Her voice was ripped raw by her silent attempts to seek help. The cloth in her mouth tasted of dirt and sweat, she tried desperately hard not to vomit as it crept its way further towards the back of her throat.

Her blood dripped onto the lilac flowers as pain shot through her groin. It felt as if she were being torn in two, ripped apart from the inside.

Annabel felt numb.

Her eyes filled as she let out another silent cry. She noticed, as if in a dream, a single diamond hair comb fall to the floor. The sparkling jewels landed face down in the mud.

Just as her vision was fading the hand on her face fell away. She turned her head the second she was able, spitting out the rancid cloth and sucking desperately at the warm air. As it hit the back of her starving throat, she heaved the entire contents of her stomach out onto the ground.

She felt violated.

She wanted to scream, to get back to the safety of her home and lie in her warm bedchamber. To cocoon herself in expensive fabric and forget this had ever happened.

She pictured her mother and father, how they might look at her once this had come to light. Would they be angry with her? Would they think she had played a part in the unfolding of these events?

She tried to picture her future husband, imagining what he might look like, how his brow would crease up in concern for her. She was meant to be announcing her engagement that evening. Would she still be a worthy wife? That was everything she had been brought up to be but she was no longer pure. No longer perfect.

These thoughts crossed through her mind like a lighting flash, quick but searingly painful. It was the shame, bubbling like molten lava in her gut, which stuck around to haunt her.

With the man's breath receding slightly as he stood up, Annabel mustered every ounce of strength she still possessed and rose to her feet, stumbling through the trees as fast as possible.

Pain stabbed her every fiber, whilst her clothes were ripped and soiled beyond recognition. None of this mattered in that moment; all she knew was that she must get as far away from there as possible before it happened again.

Her breathing was dangerously quick, forcing her to run bent double.

She had only gotten a few yards when a second man grabbed her by the waist and flung her over his shoulder. This time she found her voice. Filling her lungs she let out the loudest scream her raw throat was able to conjure.

It was still not enough.

She had run in the wrong direction, going further into the forest, definitely too far now to be heard from the sunny park beyond the trees.

Annabel glanced down at the man holding her. He seemed to move in the fast, agile way that suggested youth. She kicked out with more vigour, trying desperately to hit the place she knew would make him fall to the ground.

Eventually, her foot flew true.

He screamed in agony and crumpled, dropping Annabel who fell hard, knocking the wind out of her and ruining her advantage.

Scrambling back to her feet, she was wrenched onto the floor and another white hot pain shot through her temple. With this blow her body slackened and once more, everything went black.

Chapter Two

When Annabel opened her eyes only a matter of minutes later she was lying on her back, her feet now bound with the same rough rope as her wrists. Two male voices were laughing off to her right, the scent of damp earth close to her face.

"I dunno...people'll look for her."

His voice was uneven, thick with testosterone and self-importance. The other man coughed, loosening phlegm in his throat. Annabel heard him spit it onto the floor, it landed beside her head and she squeezed her eyes closed, tears leaking out of the corners.

"They won't find 'er."

"She's from the big 'ouse, they might."

"Yeah, the big 'ouse...think of the reward son! We got ourselves a fortune."

"Then let's take her back."

"NO! Not now, we'll wait for the reward to grow, take her to the village -"

"But when she gets back, she'll tell her folks where we are."

The rough hand grabbed Annabel's hair, pulling her up

into a seated position. The pain tore at her already sore head and she screamed. The man tied the same piece of dirty material over her eyes as before, still covered in her own sweat and vomit. It made her eyes sting as the tears now flowed even faster, desperate to remove the invading substances.

"SHUT UP!" the man yelled as she cried out again. He threw her back to the ground with a laugh. "She'll be fun while we 'ave her, control over the big 'ouse – our family's 'bout to be raised up son. We'll be lords before the years out."

Both men laughed obscenely.

"We'll be able to buy our own big 'ouse."

With that statement still ringing in the air, Annabel was picked up and thrown onto the back of a large horse. She felt one of the men jump up behind her. His boot collided with her back as he drew his leg around the animal. Annabel coughed as fresh pain bloomed from the area. The cold, cracked leather of the reins smacked rhythmically into her face as she lay helplessly against the moist fur. Blind and powerless, nausea rose up her throat. She fought to keep the bile behind her lips while tears dampened her hair.

How long had it been?

It felt like a year had passed. Surely people would be missing her by now. Annabel could only hope the police were as good as they claimed to be and would find her swiftly.

Someone must have seen her leave the park and not

return.

Someone must have heard her scream.

Anger now burst through her thick and fast, surprising even herself with its sheer intensity. She would see these men hang.

Some hours later, the steady rhythm of the horse stopped as the reins were pulled fiercely back. The horse let out its own quiet noise of complaint. Annabel was pushed from its back, landing with a thump on the bare ground. She coughed and spluttered for several seconds before regaining the ability to breathe. No sooner had she found breath, a stale lump of bread was shoved in her mouth.

"Eat." A clipped command, before the footfalls of the two men retreated.

Annabel chewed and swallowed, the bread soaking up the last precious traces of moisture in her mouth. It tasted disgusting, the claggy, floury texture of it fought its way into her throat and almost lodged itself there permanently. She wretched as the footsteps grew closer once more. Something heavy was dropped to the ground. The gentle trickle of a stream could be heard and within a few minutes the crackling of a fire, although the flames were too far away for Annabel to benefit from their warmth. She rolled over to see how far away the stream was. That's when she remembered she had been temporarily blinded.

The movement caused more pain to flare up all over her body and she stifled a moan. Listening to her attacker's voices, realising they were a few yards away and thus may be unable to see her, Annabel inched away from them. Her progress was not fast for her feet and hands were still tightly bound. However, with her first slight movement the many layers of her expensive outfit rustled, alerting the men to her escape. Their laughter ceased and she could hear them walking towards her. The dry leaves and twigs snapped beneath their feet. Annabel's breathing quickened. She was both bound and wounded.

She didn't stand a chance.

She squirmed backwards without gaining any real distance. Her blindfold was wrenched away. Her eyes, now unaccustomed to sight, could only make out the silhouetted shape of a man. The darkness prevented her seeing his features but his breath, so close to her face, was vile.

His laughter echoed around the forest. Annabel looked around frantically for an escape, knowing it was futile. The man laughed further as she struggled. Yanking her into a seated position he poured water on her face. Annabel coughed, desperately trying to suck the sustenance into her mouth. She only managed a few drops. Laughing again, he threw her back to the ground.

"I'll watch 'er. You sleep," the elder of the two men said in a gruff voice from a few feet away. The silhouetted frame nodded slightly and retreated back to the fire. The hunched shadow of the elder man came quickly into view and Annabel moved back.

"Was'a matter princess?" he crooned. He ran a finger lightly down her neck. His grip tightened around her enormous necklace. The movement was so fast she jumped, drawing in a hurried breath. The man tugged and Annabel yelped, her head jerking forward. The craftsmanship of the piece was too good to be broken. With an almost animalistic growl he forced her face to the ground and undid the necklace. The gems clicked against each other as he pocketed it.

Annabel shrank away the second he relinquished his hold on her, hoping beyond anything that the ground itself would take her into its arms and spare her the misery of another touch from this man. As if noticing Annabel's fear he laughed, a deep scratchy sound that filled her heart with dread.

"Y-you don't know what you're doing. My father will-"

"Will wha'?" the man jeered, his face mere inches from hers. Annabel swallowed. The lump of bread was still wedged inside her bone dry throat. Her breath racing past it burnt, making further speech impossible. The man laughed again and patted her cheek in an absurd mockery of kindness. He pushed her to the ground so hard she spluttered in shock. She felt her other splendid jewels being torn from her body.

"Stay 'ere or I'll kill ya," he whispered once the last of her finery had been removed. She was left only in her now torn dress and a single diamond hair comb the darkness had concealed. Perhaps Mother Nature was on her side after all.

That night was the longest of Annabel's life. Her heart continued to beat at double speed, pounding the blood around her body so she could feel it hammering against her temples. It was as if the organ was getting in as many beats as possible, in case they were her last.

Annabel's limbs were weak and tired beyond belief, yet her brain refused to sleep. It wasn't until dawn was finally cresting the horizon, both men having inched back further towards the fire, that Annabel's eyes finally drifted closed and she slipped off the edge of consciousness. There, at least, the men couldn't hurt her.

Chapter Three

The minutes grew into hours, the hours into days, until they blurred into one continuous nightmare. Every night they threw Annabel down, forcing stale bread into her unwilling mouth and filling her with water so quickly it made her choke. The brief spells of unconsciousness were her one relief. The sound of the river running beside them was the only constant Annabel could find. Her heightened sense of hearing clung to the noise desperately, convinced that should the sound cease to exist then so, in turn, should she.

Panicked, Annabel awoke one morning to silence. The gentle trickle of the stream had vanished. She was lying flat on a cold surface, the strong stench of urine filling her nostrils. With a scream, her eyes flew open.

Annabel tried to sit up but a hand pushed her back down to the floor. Pain shot through every muscle like fire. She screamed and kicked out her legs despite the hurt, noticing within seconds they were no longer bound. A strong, warm hand covered her mouth. At this she went limp. She knew where this was going so she resigned herself to it, tears sliding silently into her hair. Several seconds went by but still nothing happened.

"Shh...can't wake 'em," a voice next to her kept muttering over and over again. The hand moved from her mouth and began stroking her hair rhythmically away from her face. Glancing around, Annabel noticed she was lying on the grimy floor of a stable. Two surprisingly clean plough horses stood in the corner, crunching on a pile of fresh hay. Thick cobwebs spanned the length of the ceiling, swaying in a slight breeze whilst dust floated in a thin beam of light coming from a window mostly hidden up in the rafters. A rickety ladder, tied together with frayed string, rested on the edge of a second floor - a loft of sorts. Directly opposite her stood a muddy stable door, the imprints of large horse shoes had splintered the wood.

Annabel curled into a tight ball. She was still wearing the same dress she had left the manor in an immeasurable amount of days before, although it was soiled and torn beyond recognition. Adding to her gruesome appearance, dried blood covered both her clothes and skin.

"Okay, okay. Billy here," she heard beside her ear. It sounded like the voice of a child - innocent and reassuring. She reached up to the hand stroking her hair, tears now coming thick and fast from her eyes as sobs racked her body from head to toe.

"Okay, okay," the voice repeated over and over again.

Annabel drifted in and out of consciousness that day, drinking water that Billy held up to her expectant lips. She didn't eat anything and she didn't speak. She just lay there, her eyes squeezed shut as if by pretending this was all a bad dream, she would eventually wake up on the morning of her eighteenth birthday, when her life was supposed to have begun.

The gentle noises of the horses always brought her back to her harsh reality.

As dawn peeked its way back through a high, filthy window, Annabel opened her eyes and turned to look at Billy for the first time. What she saw made her gasp.

The person stroking her hair was an adult, probably even older than herself, although it was impossible to tell by how much. His eyes were fixed in a vacant expression she had only ever seen on the children from the asylum.

Billy was plump, whilst still having the appearance of being grossly underfed. He had a round, pink face and white blonde hair that looked as though it had been cut with a blunt knife. His eyes were small but a beautiful shade of hazel that glittered as they fixed on Annabel's.

None of the opinions regarding these people were favourable in her society. Yet Billy had been the one helping her. He was probably the reason she was still something close to alive. He had been kind when there was no need for him to be, something that bemused Annabel completely. She gripped Billy's hand tightly whilst he continued to pat her head. Her heart ached with fondness for his unwarranted compassion.

"You like horses?" he asked after a while, shattering the heavy silence. His voice was deep but playful.

Annabel nodded. Billy stood up, walking over to a chestnut horse with a white star between its eyes.

"This Troy."

He caressed the horse's nose, muttering into its ear. Troy nuzzled back into his hand as if he understood. Billy walked over to the other horse, a palomino with massive hair covered hooves.

"This Buck."

Annabel's heart sank as she recognised the horse. It was the very horse that had brought her here. The very horse upon which she had shed a countless amount of tears, had suffered countless amounts of abuse. This could only mean one thing...they had made it to the village.

For Billy's sake, she smiled. It was a tight smile, an expression that felt wrong on her usually scornful face. Her eyes were the only part that gave away her fear. Oblivious, Billy continued to pet the horses with obvious attachment. Whilst he was grubby and un-kept, the horses literally shone. He tended to them with such affection it made Annabel's racing heart bleed. She hoped the stable boys at the manor had half the skill this man possessed.

As they sat in the gloom, Annabel's fear rising with every inhalation of her breath, the stable door creaked open. Her eyes widened whilst Billy leapt to his feet with surprising agility and shrank into the corner closest to the horses.

Through a thin gap a young woman squeezed inside. She was short in stature and like Billy, appeared under-fed. However, as Annabel's eyes ran over the length of her frame she saw a grotesquely round abdomen protruding from her emaciated frame. She seemed frightened and upon noticing Annabel's gaze, dropped a small hand-ful of something on the floor before leaving as fast as her pregnancy would allow her.

Annabel's eyes remained wide, her breathing once more on the verge of panic. Seeing the young woman, so close in age to Annabel, scared her more than anything else she had seen thus far.

Was this to be her new future?

"I can't - I can't," she muttered almost inaudibly.

Billy crept back over to her from his refuge, holding out what looked to be a small roll of stale bread. Annabel ignored him, still locked in fear.

"I can't - can't stay here. This isn't me. I cannot stay here!"

Her voice exploded from her unexpectedly. A rich fire had begun to burn once more in her gut.

"Shh it's -"

"Do not dare to tell me it is okay! It is far from okay!"

Billy shrank back into the wall, his instinctual response to raised voices. The fear on his face instilled a tender feeling in Annabel's heart that was mixed with a nagging sort of pain - compassion and guilt. The new feelings brought on a new round of anger as she tried to suppress them.

"Don't look at me like that! I don't belong here, I have to leave!"

She stood, watching Billy as his large frame trembled ever so slightly, with a downcast expression on his face. Instinct told her to go to him yet the fire in her belly told her to run - to get out of this village whilst she still had the courage.

"I'm sorry. Thank you for everything," she whispered as she turned on her heel, leaving him sitting there on the floor, confusion evident on his features.

Annabel walked quickly towards the door and thoughtlessly swung it open. The cool air slapped her across the face, greeting her with its fresh open arms as it blew the rags of her expensive gown around her battered body.

Annabel stepped outside.

From the moment her foot landed on the dirt of what appeared to be a thin alleyway, the hair on her neck stood on end.

She was being watched.

She felt eyes piercing through her skin yet, look as she might, she couldn't locate their gleam. Annabel had always loved being watched. The thrill of someone's gaze upon her form had entranced her since childhood and had made her senses exceptionally sharp. This feeling was different.

This feeling was sinister.

She felt almost as if the eyes were willing her back inside her prison, warning her of a consequence she did not yet know. However Annabel, in her high society arrogance, chose to ignore their warning and took another step. Her pace increased as her confidence grew, until she could see the light of an open space just beyond the alley.

A door slammed.

So locked in her own thoughts and panic Annabel jumped, a small screech leaping out of her lungs before she could clamp a slender hand to her mouth.

Footsteps could be heard growing closer to where Annabel foolishly stood in the open. She pressed herself against the wall but there was nowhere for her to hide, she stuck out like a sore thumb. The smell of her alone would have given her away.

An elderly woman, with hair the colour and texture of straw, rounded the corner, fixing her eyes upon Annabel immediately. She didn't speak, she simply glared. The slow pace of her stride seemed almost arrogant but somehow all the more terrifying.

Annabel whipped her head left and right trying to find an escape, but there was nowhere to go. The opposite end of the alley was blocked off by a ruined wall, presumably what had attached the stable to a long fallen house. Someone with more ability than her could have scaled it but she knew she didn't stand a chance.

As a last ditch resort Annabel drew herself up to her full height and pointed her chin to the air. She looked down her nose at the woman standing directly in front of her, ignoring the vice like grip she now had on Annabel's arm.

"I implore you to let go of my arm," Annabel stated with as much authority as she could muster. Her voice shook slightly with nerves. "I am the daughter of Lord and Lady Hoddington, you do not wish to harm me."

The elderly woman simply laughed. Spit flew from her mouth as she did so, landing on Annabel's alabaster skin. The grip on her arm tightened and the woman began walking again, pulling Annabel along behind her.

"Let me go!" Annabel cried, her authority now lost in panic. The woman possessed much more strength than Annabel would have thought. Her shoulder ached where she dragged her arm at an awkward angle, the socket clicking as it teetered on the edge of dislocation.

Without thinking Annabel struck out her free hand until it collided with her captors head. Her foot followed, kicking the back of the woman's knees and causing her to fall to the ground with a surprised gasp of pain.

The woman appeared fragile as she lay sprawled in the dirt, yet Annabel felt no pity. After only a matter of seconds, she started to run.

Her feet thundered along the ground as she fled. Her breathing deafeningly loud as it rasped from her lungs. The second she stepped out of the alley she collided with another form. Both of them went down, crashing against the ground with a thud. Annabel tried to scramble to her feet but arms were upon her, keeping her on the floor. She tried to glance around, frantically searching for an escape. She remembered the stream above all else, thinking of it as her one safe haven amongst this nightmare, but there was no water in sight.

"Keep 'er down. Hurt her. Make sure she never runs away again. You can take what you like from 'er."

The command was harsh and the arms holding her stiffened as if in fear. They clearly had their own orders to follow and their own consequences should they disobey. Seizing her one brief window of opportunity Annabel made a dive for a close by line of trees. Everything else was just a blur to her.

"Please. I'm Annabel Hoddingon," she tried as she was grabbed once again. A hand collided with her cheek. Her head whipped back with the force of the slap and she stumbled. Another pair of arms caught her and threw her to the ground again where a third set of hands tore at her rags and skin. Despite their fear, these people were greedy and she was still wearing a fortune.

"They will find me!" Annabel screamed. "My father - my father will have you killed -"

The hands only stilled for a brief millisecond at the threat before they continued to remove the remains of her former glory. As the final shred of clothing left her body she became aware of a strong odour of liqueur and sweat. She froze as the other attackers backed away.

Her feet kicked out with new vigour. Her voice reaching an ear splitting pitch as she screamed, in vain, for help but it was to no avail.

It was happening again.

Laughter echoed around the square as pain tore at her every cell. The worse it got, the more the spectators seemed to cheer. It was as if they were watching a sick kind of game.

More people seemed to gather as word spread around the village. Their voices rose above Annabel's anguished screams as they held aloft her expensive fabric. At some point a foot made contact with her face, whether by accident or purpose she would never know. Her teeth sank into her bottom lip and the copper taste of blood filled her mouth.

"No," she whimpered. "My father will - my father will - he'll find you."

She managed to choke out the threat between breaths. Tears filled her eyes as the cold wind pimpled her naked body.

When it was finished there was a final explosion of laughter. As the man rose to his feet he was patted on the back as if he had won first prize in a competition.

Screams of terror quickly filled Annabel's ears as her original attackers pounced. They pummeled their way through the crowd, taking back Annabel's fabric – the skin of her former life. They seemed to control everyone. The fear was so thick she could taste it.

Annabel's vision clouded as the crowd dissipated, leaving her bruised, bloodied and humiliated on the cold ground of the village square.

She could still feel distant eyes upon her but, despite this, she hadn't the energy to continue her escape. It seemed this was her life now and she was unable to flee.

With this realisation festering within her, echoing around her mind until she felt crazed by the thought, she curled into a tight ball, her hands clawing into the bare dirt beneath her. Her nails broke with a sharp scratch of pain as she tried to find some kind of release for the anger and sorrow tearing her apart. Sobs ripped through her lungs so violently she could barely find the breath to stay alive. Part of her didn't even want to.

When her body could take no more and pain began to bring her slowly into the comfort of unconsciousness, she felt something light and warm being draped over her - a blanket of some sort she assumed - before she was heaved into the air by a slender yet strong pair of arms. She tensed but didn't have the strength to struggle.

"Shh."

His voice was almost musical.

Annabel took comfort in his warmth, curling up tighter within the thin blanket. A musty smell of clean skin, earth and soap filled her nostrils, only adding to her sense of safety. Wrapped in this foreign comfort, sleep took her under its wing within a matter of seconds.

Chapter Four

Annabel only became semiconscious as she was placed on the ground of the stable. Straw was piled up around her in the fashion of a large nest whilst cold water was dabbed across her face, arms and feet, soothing her pain somewhat.

Hazel eyes swam in front of her blurred vision and when she came too properly - an immeasurable amount of time later - it was to find Billy staring back at her. Once more he was rhythmically stroking her hair, in a gesture that had come to symbolise kindness for her.

She groaned as pain flooded her body all over. Her lips felt cracked and swollen as she tried to speak, the movement causing a fresh bead of blood to trickle down her chin. Billy immediately wiped it away and smiled at her.

"You okay," he muttered, placing a tender, fatherly kiss on the top of her head. She squeezed her eyes shut but still a few tears escaped her lids.

"No - no I'm not," she croaked, her voice too thick with grief to utter more than a whisper.

"You will be. Promise." Billy whispered back, his eyes full of purity and innocence.

Suddenly the door banged open, shattering the peace.

Annabel leapt up despite her wounds and nakedness, crawling to the farthest corner in the hope of disappearing in the shadows. Billy followed her, cowering at her side. Once more he stroked his hand along her hair, in a way of reassuring himself as much as Annabel.

In the doorway stood two men. They were both exactly the same height and build, although one was clearly older than the other. The younger had coarse, chestnut hair, almost identical in shade to the horse Billy had identified as Troy. His teeth were chipped and blackened; his skin scabbed and rough looking. The older of the men had grey hair with only some remnants of his former chestnut shade. His eyes were so dark they were almost black. Their features were identical, meaning they could only be father and son.

As the scent of liqueur washed over her face like a harsh wind Annabel began to shake in terror. For the last few hours, the dream like memory of those arms wrapped around her still fresh in her mind, she had believed herself something close to safe - believed that in here at least they wouldn't get her.

Both of the men approached, smiling with pure triumph. They reached her at the exact same time. Annabel winced as the younger man knelt down and raised a hand. He pulled out the remaining diamond hair comb still loosely secured in her hair. Unencumbered, the strands fell freely over her face. Peeking out from beneath this messy curtain, she saw the elder man stood at her feet.

Billy whimpered. Annabel had eaten so little over the last week, she prayed it meant she was close to death. Billy began to howl as the silence continued to grow.

"Shut up idiot!" the younger man yelled, drawing back his fist and smashing it into Billy's face with such force he was thrown back. He stumbled up, sobbing pathetically, and crawled towards the horses, holding his bleeding face in his hands. Blood seeped out from between his chubby fingers.

Annabel lay limp on the floor, trying to hold back her wails of disgust as the younger man ran a finger down her cheek.

"Papa told me 'bout you runnin'. You won't do tha' again, understand?"

Annabel squeezed her eyes shut as tightly as she could, hoping beyond anything they would leave. The fingers on her face tightened around her chin.

"UNDERSTAND?!" he yelled.

Annabel nodded. Her head bobbing up and down made her hair swing lifelessly from her scalp.

"Right, now," he paused for dramatic effect. His tone suggested he was scolding an unruly child. "Where'd ya put your pretty jewels? Didn' think ya could stay 'ere for nothin' did ya?"

"I - I -" Annabel stuttered, confused why they were asking these questions. Wasn't he the one that took them?

"WHERE DID YOU PUT 'EM!" he screamed, spraying spit in her face.

Annabel shook with terror. "They were - they were

t-taken. You saw it - I don't know." She glanced at the man who glared at her, licking his lips slightly as if he were gazing upon a particularly juicy piece of meat. There was humour in his dark eyes. They knew exactly what had happened, he simply wanted to see her get hurt further. Annabel's stomach twisted with such violent disgust she was nearly sick.

"Those greedy sons of -" the younger man began as he looked at his father, a glint in his eye too. This was, to them, just another game and she was their toy.

Before Annabel could so much as blink the man's hand flew through the air and crashed into her face. She was thrown backwards just like Billy, her head smacking on the slimy stone wall. Both men laughed as she let out a pained cry. They left with only the echo of their laughter to haunt her dark thoughts.

Annabel curled back into her ball, rocking herself slowly as a fresh round of sobs escaped her lips, ripping apart her already raw throat.

More than once she noticed someone stood in the open doorway, come to stare at the sight of her so helplessly humiliated, but none of them came in to help. Every one of them had the same glint of terror in their eyes.

Billy tried to approach on several occasions but he was scared as well. The noise escaping Annabel now was of the deepest pain and he had seen too much of that in his lifetime already.

Huddled in the corner Annabel rocked herself into a blissfully numb state, where she couldn't feel the pain or humiliation as badly anymore. She shivered as the cool air brushed over her. Grouping around on the floor for something to cover herself, her fingers found the blanket which still held the soapy scent of safety.

Annabel remained like this for hours, until the same young woman as the day before snuck into the gloomy enclosure. She dumped a bundle of cloth on the floor once she was just across the threshold and fled, as if scared by the very sight of the stable's prisoners.

Sitting up slowly, gasping as the pain stabbed through her with renewed vigour, Annabel grabbed at the pile of rags eagerly. Uncaring and wanting only to be covered, she stepped into the rough, mud brown dress. It looked as if it had been badly homemade by the cheapest fabric to hand. Almost medieval in its simplicity, it hung off of her slim frame in a horrible manner Annabel was not used to. The coarse fabric scraped against her already tender skin, making it itch almost immediately. Nevertheless, the dress was warm and hung down to her bare feet, thus covering most of her shamed body. As she stood up, some pieces of stale bread rolled out of the folds of material.

She noticed Billy had come back over to her from his position by the horses and started devouring one of the deformed pieces. Annabel did the same, neither tasting nor feeling the bread as she ate. After their humble meal, the two reluctant roommates crawled to their separate slimy corners, losing themselves again in their individual misery.

The next two days continued in the same heavy si-

lence, only to be broken by the scarce delivery of bread
and water.

During this time neither Annabel nor Billy saw the
two brutal men again, although she had often heard their
shouting voices from nearby, causing her to tremble in
fright each time. One such argument involved a woman
shouting about carelessness. She seemed to think Annabel
would bring them misfortune, as surely people were already looking for her. This argument had ended with the
heavy thwack of a fist hitting supple flesh and a whimper
of pain from a woman clearly used to abuse. When the
pregnant girl re-entered the stable that evening, half of
her face was swollen up in a vivid bruise.

For a few lonely hours every day Billy left the stable,
going out to watch the horses when they were being used
and doing, from what Annabel gathered from his broken
speech, to be heavy lifting and chores no one else wanted
to do. She felt a little queasy that just over a week ago
she had been the one giving out the orders for people like
him. He came back into the stable each night with barely enough energy to eat the little amount of food he was
permitted, before crawling back to his corner and falling
asleep. Annabel however, did not try to leave the stable
again. Every time she so much as considered it her bones
turned cold, her body shivering with the memory of her
last, failed attempt. It seemed, from the overheard snip-
pets of conversation, they were deciding what to do with
her. The men wanted, as they had said in the forest, to
keep her here until the manor asked for a high enough

reward for her return. This idea gave Annabel a small amount of hope. Perhaps, if she sat tight, she would be able to go home after all.

Chapter Five

On the third day the monotonous routine was broken when a young girl with the now familiar chestnut hair – all be it a slightly more fiery shade and frizzy texture - came into the stable. She passed Annabel bread with a thin layer of dripping. This was a treat she had not sampled since her arrival and she devoured it greedily, before looking up at the girl still standing in front of her. She had a short, petite frame and round face. She appeared almost childlike although there was a haunted pain in her dark eyes. Her small hands were scarred and calloused.

"Come wi' me," she whispered, glancing over her shoulder without so much as an introduction. "Quick."

"They're watching me," Annabel whispered in a tiny voice. "I can't leave."

"They won't tell on you if you're with me. Trust me."

Annabel simply stayed put. She had seen too much in the past few days to begin trusting someone that easily. The young girl rolled her eyes, placing her hands on her hips in a gesture far too old for her meagre years.

"I'm not trickin' you. Do I look like I'd do tha'? Come on." She sounded impatient, as if she had already seen far too much resistance in her short life. "I lived 'ere me whole life. I know wha' I'm doing."

The temptation to go outside, to shake free of the oppressive stable, of the constant stench of urine and animals, was too much to resist, no matter how frightened she was. Very slowly, like a horse at risk of bolting, Annabel rose to her feet.

Her head spun as she staggered over the uneven floor. Pieces of straw stuck to the exposed soles of her feet, they crackled with every step she took. She felt weak and swollen, her limbs aching. Annabel hesitated for a long time in the open doorway. Her feet lingered on the threshold as her eyes ran the length of the gloomy ally. The young girl didn't even notice her absence until she was almost out in the open, at which point she spun sharply around.

"Come on," the girl seemed to be finding Annabel's behaviour almost humorous.

Tentatively Annabel placed one foot in front of the other, making her way as slowly as possible across the ground she had walked again and again in her nightmares. She glanced over her shoulder so often it appeared as if she had a twitch.

Upon exiting the street Annabel raised her hands over her face, the bright sunlight sending a sudden shock through her as it hit her eyes. Her heart rate increased once again as she imagined hands on her. Feeling these ghostly touches she shivered, running her own fingers over herself in the attempt to shake them off. She stumbled in her panic and nearly screamed. The small, warm hand of the girl wrapped itself around Annabel's shoulders just before her lungs could let out the sound of her fear. There was a look of the deepest concern in her dark eyes as the girl steered her forward.

Annabel could only assume it was this young girl's turn to watch her now.

Despite this knowledge, despite the fact she was still just a prisoner and the girl her new guard, the pleasure of being outside was incredible. She sucked greedily at the fresh air, absorbing the different smells and sounds of the nearby forest as eagerly as she had devoured the bread but ten minutes earlier.

After a few feet, her eyes became accustomed to the light. Glancing around her with higher awareness she saw that she was being led out of a small medieval looking village. There were about ten houses built in a large, dusty clearing made entirely from earth and wood, the centre piece of which was an unlit fire pit built in the middle.

A flash of remembrance - herself lying exposed on that very ground - came into her head and she shut her eyes against the humiliation. The memory burnt even hotter behind her closed lids, forcing her to reopen them.

There were cages dotted around the clearing, made in a similar manner to the stable ladder. They housed various small animals. The larger of the animals were tied to trees and posts. A few people were outside, mainly women on their daily chores, plucking chickens or sweeping dirt out of their rickety front doors. All of them wore clothes in shades of brown or grey, in the same coarse fabric as her own. Only some wore knitted shawls or coats of animal skin. It looked as if they used every part of the animals they killed, much unlike the manor where it was custom to leave much more than they ate.

Many of the villagers glanced towards her but they all looked away again. Some of them Annabel now recognised as having walked past the stable to ogle at her shamed form. She made sure to linger on their faces a little longer, fixing them with a look of undiluted disgust - an expression she had perfected well in her upper class role.

Once they passed through the village centre Annabel heard the slow trickle of running water. Her spirits soared and her throat clenched in thirst. It took everything she had not to sprint towards the sound.

They walked a short distance inside the trees before Annabel saw a magnificent waterfall, trickling down into a clear blue stream, surrounded by the last bluebells of the spring. It was in-comprehensible that somewhere so stunning could be so close to such misery.

Annabel clambered down the bank, scrapping her bare feet on the rocks and immediately plunged her face beneath the stream's glistening surface. She felt the cool water lap around her temples and saw her hair splay out around her, dancing in the slow current. She sucked the liquid into her body greedily, until she was forced to re-surface, gasping for breath. When Annabel looked back into the stream she saw a small cloud of dirt floating away from where her face had just been and realised how filthy she must be. She had not bathed since her last day at the manor. Dirt covered her body from head to toe and her skin was rubbed raw from her attempts at scrubbing away the blood, using only the coarse material of her dress. Shedding the filthy garment, she lowered herself into the stream, completely submerging her body. She gasped as the cool water soothed her frail frame. She was covered in bruises and had turned waxy and pale from the severe change in her diet. She saw blood that had been dry for over a week peel away from her skin, along with more dirt than she believed possible for one person to accumulate. She came up to the surface once more feeling a heavy sense of relief. Despite this new external sense of cleanliness she still felt dirty on the inside. No matter how clean her skin was, she knew she always would.

The entire time the young girl was sat facing Annabel with humour evident on her youthful face.

"'aving fun?" she asked. Annabel smiled back, for the first time in what felt like a lifetime.

"Name's Patsy," the girl continued. "Trevor's girl, I think you met 'im."

She said the latter with a sneer of obvious hatred. A sliver of cold fear slid down Annabel's throat at finally having a name for her attacker.

"Did you wanna use this?" Patsy reached into her apron, withdrawing a lumpy grey substance. "It's soap, tho' not like you know it I'm sure."

She placed it on the side of the pool and Annabel snatched it up, lathering it over her entire body almost violently. It still smelled like the animal fat used to make it although Annabel didn't care. As she scrubbed she felt how her bones now stuck out a little further than usual. The soap stung her skin, turning it a vivid, patchy shade of red.

Remembering her hair she lathered soap there as well, working her fingers through it over and over again in an attempt to detangle the once glorious strands. She felt the hair smoothen under the water and placed the significantly diminished soap back onto the bank. Patsy put it away again and motioned to a small pile of clothes Annabel hadn't realised she was carrying.

"Put this on when you're done."

Patsy gazed intently into Annabel's face, closely searching for any hint she would make a break for freedom. Even with the renewed energy the cool water had granted her, she still felt too weak to run. Besides, where would she go? It was at least a few days back to the park and she had no way of finding food. Her tutor hadn't deemed survival skills appropriate.

After about twenty minutes she clambered out of the stream, covering her body with her hands. As quick as she could she crawled into her new clothes. They stuck to her still wet skin. She found herself wearing a grey dress of the same rough fabric as her old one. There was also an apron, similar to the one Patsy was wearing, that reached the hem of her dress, with two wonky pockets sewn onto the front.

Although still of the same fabric, the clean dress felt luxuriously soft compared to her former one. She realised now she was clean how much she must have smelt. Unthinking she threw her old dress into the stream, watching as it floated away.

"What'd ya do that for?" Patsy scorned, jumping to her feet and chasing after it. She fished it out of the stream when it got caught on a protruding rock a few feet from where Annabel sat.

"It was filthy and disgusting, why keep it?"

The look on Patsy's face was tinged with anger as she sat back down with the dripping garment.

"I didn't 'ave to bring you 'ere. You could try an' make me life easier. If I got found out I'd be beaten to within an inch of me life. Think next time."

Annabel narrowed her eyes, anger flaring up within her as she fixed her gaze on Patsy's face. Who was this girl to tell her off?

Remembering where she was and with whom, her arrogance dissipated.

"Sorry," Annabel croaked. The rarely used word sounded strange in her voice.

"I am Miss – I mean, I am Annabel, Annabel Maria Hoddington."

Patsy smiled. "Nice t' meet ya. It's okay 'bout the dress I mean – jus' remember next time. Things don' just turn up 'ere, someone has to make 'em. It gets pretty rough in winter too, you'll wan' all the layers ya can get."

Annabel's stomach sank with the thought of still being here in the winter. And yet, her imagination halted when she tried to picture herself in the drawing rooms of the manor. She almost felt like she no longer belonged with that society now.

She was impure and tainted.

The hope of salvation diminished every day she stayed unfound in the woods. Why weren't her parents looking for her? Had she just been given up for dead?

"I was thinkin'," Patsy said after a while. "I know they keep ya pretty locked up but Mum can't sit in wait every day. We could do with some 'elp. We can always find somethin' for you to do."

"What, clean?" Annabel scoffed. "I've never cleaned anything in my life."

"You'll 'ave to learn. No-one likes that you're 'ere but makin' yourself known might jus' make it better."

Annabel had to admit, that stung. No-one liked her. But people always liked her. This time her hot temper boiled over.

"You have no right talking to me like that!" she spat; with the same scornful tone she reserved for the maids back at the manor. "I am the daughter of Lord and Lady Hoddington, betrothed to the heir to the largest fortune in England, if you know what's good for you, you'll learn your place."

Patsy folded her arms across her small chest in her own firm resistance.

"You ain't at home now Missy, don' get bossy with me. Papa won't let you leave now. There's no gettin' ya own way here. You're nothin' special no more."

Annabel trembled in defeat. The lack of control made

her feel weak and useless. Without another word Patsy took her arm, a little more forcefully than what was necessary, and steered her towards the stable. It wasn't until they got inside that Patsy let go of her. Annabel crawled into the corner and curled up into her familiar ball, tears falling unwillingly now she was back in her prison.

Chapter Six

Annabel did not look up when she heard the door open sometime later. A cold breeze floated over her, bringing with it the smell of fresh bread. In the end, Annabel's hunger got the better of her and she peeled her eyes from the slimy wall to focus on the figure now struggling across the floor. Her swollen stomach seemed to weigh her down. As Annabel watched it appeared to move ever so slightly as the child within it writhed.

As the woman stooped, Annabel simply watching from the floor, she groaned in suppressed pain. Patsy appeared silhouetted in the open door way, as if sensing the woman's anguish. She jumped into action as if kindness were as easy to her as breathing. Throwing an arm around the woman's emaciated frame she removed the heavy jug from her grip.

"Go. I've got it," Patsy whispered, kissing the woman's sweaty cheek. She smiled and withdrew with a pronounced waddle to her walk. Before she made it outside she paused, leaning against the wall to take several deep breathes. Patsy rushed up to her again but the woman waved her off and continued out of the stable. Still frowning in concern, Patsy caught Annabel's gaze.

"Tha's Hetty – Tom's wife. 'e's my older brother. Brought you 'ere wi' Trevor."

Patsy seemed angry about her family connection to Tom. Annabel didn't care about this information but Patsy continued none the less.

"She's pregnant but he makes her work even harder than when she wasn't. He says it'll make his son stronger."

She looked at Annabel cautiously, desperation for affection etched in her features.

"Sorry," Patsy said when Annabel made no attempt to speak. "About earlier. I know it must be bad for you 'ere, I don't wanna make it worse...honest. It's jus', I didn't know you'd feel so bad 'bout people not likin' you. I like you though...I do. You're like - like a princess."

Patsy smiled somewhat sheepishly and Annabel knew she couldn't remain angry with this girl. She gave her a small smile back. Patsy crept forwards a little more.

"I know wha' they did to you. They don' treat me nice neither. They hate girls. We're jus' whores and housemaids to Papa and Tom. But doin' that to you, when you didn't deserve it...ain't right."

Annabel looked at Patsy in confusion. "And you think you do deserve it?"

Patsy lowered herself down to the floor, tucking her legs under her body in a subconscious effort to make herself as small as possible.

"No. Well...I guess. He's my papa. He brought me into

the world, so 'e's earned the right to do what he wants t' me. I'm not 'is favourite...friend though. Tha's good."

Her attempt at humour was hollow, it made Annabel's stomach turn.

"He should be hung," Annabel muttered.

A look of shock passed over Patsy's face but before she could act on it Billy traipsed in, leading the horses. Patsy watched him tend to them with a deep fondness in her eyes. Upon noticing Patsy Billy ran over, his face full of enthusiasm as he hugged her tightly.

"Pat!" He burrowed his head in her shoulder as a child would their mother – not that Annabel had ever done that to her mother. Patsy begun to stroke his hair away from his face with the same rhythm Billy had used on Annabel.

"Hello brother," she gave him a soft kiss on the forehead. A look of confusion crossed Annabel's face.

"He's your brother?"

Patsy looked up, still brushing back Billy's hair.

"Yeah. I guess with the yellow hair you can't tell. Daniel's the only other light haired one of us. You'd see it if you met him, Mama's kinda yellow but not like this."

Annabel smiled again, the movement felt strange on her face. The love Patsy seemed to show her brother was beautiful, even more so compared to the hate she had seen from everyone else.

"How many of you are there?" Annabel asked.

"Billy's the eldest, he's twenty six. Then there's jus' Tom and Daniel. I'm fifteen. That's not countin' all the other bastard kids he an' Tom have probably had all over the place."

A hand went reflexively to Annabel's stomach, Patsy registered the movement.

"Don't worry, he ain't fathered anythin' since me. He blames Mama but we all know it ain't her."

Patsy's young face puckered in a worry she should not have known. "He says she gave 'im tainted sons an' girls on purpose."

She planted another kiss on Billy's head, brushing his cheek with her spare hand.

"But he has Tom." Annabel spat the name out. "And – um -"

"Daniel. Yeah I know, but he wanted all boys. Tom gets everythin' they can afford; he's Papa's pride and joy. Dani was born jus' after 'im but was always very different. He was really early too, nearly died. Papa thinks he's weak 'cuz of it. Dani sings all the time as well, like an angel...to piss off Papa I reckon."

She laughed softly to herself, obviously fond of this brother too. "Dani'd sooner deck Papa than let him 'ave his way with us. He's nearly been killed so many times tryin' to help us. He's saved my skin more than once. I wish he wouldn't. He's strong, real strong, but they bound to get 'im soon. I'm – I'm scared for 'im."

Patsy looked up, the fear evident in her face for the first time. She had seemed so strong before, older than her years. Her youth shone out now.

She was barely more than a child.

Annabel sat beside her feeling more useless than ever.

She had a position of phenomenal power but here she could not use it to help even this one girl. She could think of nothing to say that would in any way ease Patsy's suffering so chose to remain silent, looking on at the two siblings wrapped in each-others tender embrace.

How did people live like this and still manage to find love within their hearts? It begged belief.

Noticing Annabel's discomfort, Patsy changed the subject.

"I'll try to bring some stuff over tomorrow, to help. You should at least 'av a thicker blanket. Maybe candles too. Make it nicer...kinda."

Annabel looked down, embarrassed for the first time about her former, privileged life. So what if she had to endure this place for a few months? These people had lived here their entire lives.

"Thank you Patsy," she murmured. There was a new, strange stirring of pity in her heart. "I'm very grateful."

"Wha's grateful mean?"

Annabel was taken aback.

"Oh, um showing that you like what someone has done or given you...I suppose."

Patsy smiled. "Then...I'm grateful you came."

She reached over and squeezed Annabel's hand. Unused to displays of physical affection Annabel froze but after a few moments felt herself relax. The warmth of this new person's touch travelled up her arm and she squeezed back, enjoying the alien sensation of closeness. After a few minutes Patsy rose to her feet and Billy began to cry, pleading with her not to leave.

"You know I gotta go Billy, I'm sorry. I'll be back soon, honest."

She gave him a motherly smile, kissed him on the cheek and walked out the door. Billy crawled back into his corner where the sound of his breathing quickly regulated as he drifted off to sleep.

Annabel leant against the wall, looking up at the dusty loft. After a moment she found her gaze once more on the splintering ladder. Forcing herself to a standing position, she set her bare feet on the jagged rungs and climbed.

At the top she found another, much smaller room. The floor was uneven and creaky, covered in at least an inch of dust. It puffed up around her with every step she took, making her nose tickle and her feet itch. The exposed rafters above her head were sloped, meaning she had to walk bent double most of the time. The only light came from a tiny window overlooking part of the forest. It was so covered in grime it was impossible to see anything more than an outline of the stunning view. Beneath this window sat several long forgotten bales of straw, becoming nothing more than food for rats.

Over the next few hours she dragged the bales across the floor, sweating with the effort, and into the right hand corner of the tiny loft. Sprinkling some of the softer hay from downstairs over the top of the older she draped it with her new apron, until she had managed to fashion a structure somewhat resembling a bed.

After this, Annabel climbed back down the ladder,

searching for anything to brighten up the place. Her search grew more thorough until she stumbled upon a group of dandelions sprouting from the mossy wall beside the door. She picked them with a sense of childish joy and put them in the battered jug, now empty of water, which had been delivered to them that day. She set the flowers on the narrow ledge below the window. Stepping back to admire the effect, just as the sun was sinking below the trees, she smiled. It was a satisfying feeling; the knowledge she had created this sanctuary, however simple, with nothing but her own hands. This must be why people worked, she thought.

Retreating to the miserable downstairs stable, Annabel tried to coax Billy into following her up the ladder, knowing they would be safer curled together on her make shift bed in the roof. At least it would be more comfortable than the floor. Yet, he refused to be away from the horses. Sighing softly, with a physical and emotional exhaustion she had never felt, Annabel climbed back up into her new bedchamber. Lifting the ladder, so no unwanted visitors could reach her, she instantly fell into a deep and dreamless sleep.

Chapter Seven

Annabel woke the next morning to a panicked voice somewhere below her. She rolled over groaning and reached down to pull her warm duvet over her shoulders. Her hand groped into thin air, scraping against the rough fabric of her medieval style dress. She groaned louder this time, as she felt the prickle of straw beneath her and remembered where she was. The panicked voice had reached a louder volume, screaming an abbreviated version of her name.

"Anna!"

Annabel poked her head over the rafters and called down. Patsy spun around sharply, letting out an audible sigh of relief.

"Thank God, I thought you'd run away or summit. Well – not that you could, really - there's a lot o' eyes on you."

Annabel lowered the ladder, swallowing her fear at that last statement. Not yet used to the narrow rungs, she slipped several times before she made it to the safety of the floor. Patsy immediately handed over another large bundle. The intoxicating smell of food made Annabel sink to her knees, ripping it open. What she found made her mouth water. There were two slices of fresh bread spread with a thick layer of dripping, a shiny red apple and a small leg of meat – a rabbit perhaps. Annabel literally jumped on the food, devouring it without so much as taking a breath. She moaned, in a way that would normally have filled her with revulsion, as the juice from the sweet apple dripped down her chin. Half way through she wrenched it away from herself, remembering Billy. She looked around - the cool, sticky juice of the apple had now dried on her face - but she couldn't find him. Registering her intentions, Patsy spoke.

"It's okay, Billy's had some already. He's out today. This is all yours."

That was all the invitation Annabel needed. She lunged on the second half with just as much vigour, polishing off every last crumb of bread and sucking on the rabbit bone until all the traces of meat had gone. When there was no more food to eat, Patsy passed over a jug full to the brim of water. Annabel guzzled this down, spilling some of it down her front in her haste.

"Thank you," she said with tears of gratification clouding her eyes.

"You really needed that, huh?" Patsy giggled, whilst understanding hung in her own intense gaze.

Both girls laughed; giddy with the simple pleasure of the moment.

"Look a' the rest." Patsy gestured to the bundle surrounding the smuggled food.

Annabel took her time unfolding these stolen gifts, allowing herself some joy at the discovery of a thick moth eaten nightdress, a new apron and a pair of crudely carved wooden clogs. The best of the bundle though, was a thick patchwork quilt, badly hand sewn in a hurry from squares of sheep wool and cow hide. Tears slowly made tracks down Annabel's cheeks. She had received more presents in her lifetime than an army of people have room for, yet this one, so full of devotion and kindness, was her favourite by far. She smiled up at Patsy who was looking a little anxious.

"Do you like it?" she whispered. Annabel nodded, unable to speak through the lump building in her throat.

"Made it meself, been smugglin' pieces of fabric for days. I saw a blanket like this in the town when I was a littelen an' always wanted to make one. I did make one for Billy a few years back. It kills me that he's in 'ere with nothing. I try to bring him things but it's right nasty when I get caught, we both get it pretty bad-"

Annabel sat listening in silence, fingering the loose threads on her new blanket. Watching Annabel's elegant fingers, Patsy began to explain the process she had gone through to make it, pointing towards various parts as she explained their conception. Her pride in the item was enviable. She held up her hands to show the small pin pricks she had gotten from using the needle without a thimble.

"Did you ever sew at home?" Patsy concluded.

"Yes," Annabel murmured, remembering with a slight blush of shame, the hours she had sat in various fancy rooms amusing herself with this pass time. "But only embroidery. Not anything functional. I had dressmakers for that."

"If I can find anythin' to do it with, can you teach me to do it proper?" Patsy's cheeks turned red with excitement and Annabel was reminded again just how young she was. She nodded, feeling it was the least she could do, considering everything Patsy had already done for her.

Annabel stood up, tied her apron around her waist and draped the nightdress and quilt around her shoulders. She went to put on the clogs but decided against it, wanting to feel the ladders rungs beneath her toes. She attempted to throw the clogs up to the second floor so both her hands would be free to climb. The first few attempts failed and Patsy joined in, making it into a bit of a game. When eventually the clogs found the upper floor, both girls cheered, laughing so hard they were soon gasping for breath. Annabel thought about how ashamed her mother would be, if she saw her acting in such a frivolous manor in company but quickly realised she didn't care.

"Follow me," she said, grabbing Patsy's hand on instinct and leading her towards the ladder.

Once at the top, Annabel located the clogs, placing them neatly beside her bed and hung the nightdress on a loose nail protruding from the exposed rafters. Her new blanket, placed with the corner turned down, added a final homely touch. Both Annabel and Patsy stood in silence for a little while, soaking in the gloomy space. Annabel watched a lone spider crawl slowly up from the bed and out a wide crack in the window. Patsy shifted her feet on the floor, the movement left marks in the thick dust.

"Are you alright?" Annabel asked, noticing a worried frown had returned to Patsy's youthful forehead. Patsy looked up, as if caught doing something she shouldn't.

"Yeah I -" she started, but her resolve crumbled and her shoulders slumped. "I dunno."

She sat down on the end of Annabel's bed, fidgeting with the ragged edge of her apron. "I'm just – I try to be strong an' that, but I'm worried about Hetty. See, she's not well. I know she's havin' a baby but I don't remember her being like this with her other kids. She's slower an' seems to be hurtin' a lot more." Patsy took a shaky breath. "She never even wanted to marry Tom – I mean, who would? She wanted Daniel but he didn't like her like that, an' he had someone else at the time, so Hetty ended up gettin' real squiffy at the pub an' had a night with Tom – she was so drunk she don't even remember it. Ended up havin' twins. Her mama and papa made her marry 'im but said she had shamed them or summit so won't even look at her now. I hate them for doing that to her. She's been left with that dog of a husband who abuses her in all kinda ways, he thinks it's her duty."

Annabel was listening in horror, her eyes wide. The more she heard about this family the more appalled she became.

"But this is absurd, surely Tom's happy? Why does he still have to abuse her? You said they already have children, right?"

"Yeah, two boys, but he wants more - lots of 'em. He jus' wants her to deliver 'im healthy sons, keep his supper on the table and 'is house clean. No romance in this village Ma'am."

This was the first time Annabel had been addressed thus for a long time, it made her cheeks colour with shame. She felt disgusted acknowledging this distinction in their classes. The things she had deemed so important in her former life were now sickeningly trivial.

There were another few moments of silence as the information Patsy had just divulged lay bare and exposed between them.

"I don't think you wanna hear 'bout my family any more – what 'bout yours? Are you very rich? You must be, Papa got a lot o' money for your things. They were very pretty."

Before she had a chance to answer, Patsy gasped and reached into her apron, making Annabel jump.

"That reminds me. I found this in the mud jus' outside the stable the other day."

She held out her hand, unfurling the fingers. It was Annabel's time to gasp now, for resting in Patsy's dry, red palm was one of Annabel's diamond encrusted hair combs. She picked it up, remembering how it had felt when the maids slipped it into her elaborately braided hair. It seemed like years ago.

Annabel held the comb up to the light, watching the familiar twinkle as the sun shone through the jewels, refracting on the wall behind her. It was a token to the quality of the piece that none of the gems had even moved. Patsy had clearly spent ages washing it, getting into every groove. Sitting next to Patsy and leaning backwards, Annabel placed this treasure in the tiny gap between the bed and the wall, then sat back up to squeeze Patsy's hand tightly in her own.

"It's very beautiful," Patsy said. "Did it cost lots?"

"I don't know. I assume so. I had four of them in my hair when I left, loads more at home though." Patsy's mouth opened in awe, she looked positively dumbstruck.

"You 'ad lots?"

"Yes, I wore jewels every day."

Patsy's mouth widened even more. Annabel felt her cheeks colour in further embarrassment, noticing how something as ordinary to her as a diamond hair comb, could cause so much disbelief. Once more, the insignificance of such a thing became startlingly apparent. Patsy's eyes glanced down towards the dusty floor.

"So – so this diamond isn't that special then? 'cuz you've got lots more."

Annabel squeezed Patsy's hand again. "No Patsy, this one is the most special one I've ever owned, thank you for rescuing it. Honestly, thank you."

Patsy smiled again, squeezing back. "Did you live in a big house?"

"Yes, it was a manor house right at the top of a big hill, overlooking the entire town."

"Wow. What's it like? I've only been to the town two times with Papa an' he covered my eyes the whole way 'til we'd got to the market, then he'd use me to take things from the stalls 'cuz I were so small at the time. You gotta tell me everythin'!"

Patsy was beside herself with excitement. Annabel talked about everything she could think of. She described the balls, including the etiquette required of her, providing examples where necessary which Patsy always attempted to copy. Next Annabel took her through a description of the entire manor, with as much detail as she could remember. Patsy listened to the whole thing with rapt attention, hanging on every word like a child being told a fairy tale before bed. After a while, a voice made its way closer to the stable, calling for Patsy. She jumped up to hurry, with much more expertise than Annabel, down the rickety ladder.

"In here!" she called.

After a few seconds Hetty came into view at the stable door, looking pained and exhausted. Patsy put a hand tenderly on Hetty's shoulder and urged her to sit down.

"No, no I can't. Tom wants me to help your mama and the boys need feeding."

Seeing Patsy's concern she added, "I'm okay, the world don't stop because you're 'aving a baby. Our men still need their chores done."

Her voice started to strain with suppressed agony and she bent at the waist slightly, closing her eyes.

"Hetty you need to rest!"

"NO! I can't rest! Tom wants things done, 'e won't have mercy if they aren't. When he wants what he wants it wouldn't matter if the baby was half way out, I would still have to do it!"

Shaking slightly she turned and forced her voice to sound light.

"Please come back to the house Patsy, I'd really like the help."

Patsy glanced up at Annabel, now making her descent from the loft. She looked haggard.

"Can you come to the house too?" she murmured, so quietly one might have missed it. "I don't think I can face her on my own, she's in agony."

As she pondered her sister in laws fate, a mirror of all their futures, tears were not evident at all in Patsy's dark eyes...instead there was hell.

Chapter Eight

As they paced their way over to the wonky house next door, Annabel became aware of a growing unease in her stomach. She was walking into the complete unknown. The further lack of control terrified her.

Following Patsy through a low wooden door, that wobbled on its handmade hinges as she opened it, Annabel found herself in a dark room with a low ceiling. The walls were made from dried mud and straw, the floor just bare earth.

Most of the room was filled by a large table with wonky legs, surrounded by a set of stools, all of it handmade. In the far right hand corner was a doorway leading to what Annabel naively assumed to be the various bedchambers. On the wall to Annabel's left was a fireplace – or rather a deep dent in the wall with a hole above it, acting as something of a chimney. A small window beside the door was the only source of light in the otherwise dim and smoky space. At the fire stooped the elder woman. Her straw-like hair was tied roughly at the nape of her neck with a worn piece of string. Annabel's heart rate increased at the very sight of her sneering, prematurely aged face. In the opposite corner Hetty was knelt on the floor, one hand still rubbing at her grotesquely out of proportion belly, her other hand deep in a rusty tub of soapy water, washing what looked like blood off of a grey dress.

"What happened?" Patsy asked, rushing to Hetty's side and taking the sodden dress out of her hand.

"Oh it's just a bit of blood, it happens sometimes when you're pregnant, it's fine," she replied, trying to sound reassuring.

"No it doesn't Hetty, you shouldn't be bleeding and you know it!"

"I've got to get these stains out before Tom sees, he can't know."

Annabel noticed that Hetty's bony hands were trembling as she worked. Feeling an out of character sense of concern Annabel rushed over as well, gently pulling at Hetty's shoulders to ease her back onto the floor.

"Get off me!" she screamed, crawling out of Annabel's grasp to the other side of the tub, her face creased in pain. "Why did you bring her here? Haven't we got enough problems?" she snapped at Patsy.

"I didn't bring her here Hetty, you know that. I'm jus' making her life better now she is."

Hetty glanced up into Annabel's face sceptically. "She ain't a stray cat you can tame Patsy. Who are you anyway?" She directed the question towards Annabel.

"Miss Annabel Hoddington, daughter of Lord Grayson and Lady Elizabeth Hoddington."

"Lord and Lady? What were they thinking? We'll all be

killed in our sleep."

"I assure you, that is not my intention. I would like to leave as much as you want me gone."

"You assure me." Hetty snorted in a scornful laugh that turned into a suppressed groan halfway. "Make yourself useful. Help the old woman with dinner."

"I have never cooked before, so I think I would be better placed with you. I'd hate to ruin dinner."

"Would you now? Well, grab one of those shirts," Hetty gestured to the large pile of clothes next to her knees. "Patsy you help your mama."

Patsy did as she was told. Going over to the fire she rested a hand on her mother's shoulder and whispered in her ear. The older woman shook off her daughter's touch with a disgruntled look. Rising to her feet, she left Patsy alone to finish the meal, picking up a large woven basket on her way. Annabel watched her leave as she begun to wash the disgustingly dirty garment in her hands. Hetty continued to scrub at her dress with growing urgency, her face creased up and crimson. Her quick breath laboured occasionally over the strongest bouts of hurt. She groaned as the pain seemed to reach its peak.

Annabel had no real knowledge of pregnancy. All the women she knew had been taken away for bed rest in the latter months. They never emerged back into society until their body had returned to as close to their former shape as possible. They certainly did not run errands and crouch on the floor to wash shirts.

A thin sheen of sweat was now glistening over Hetty's

face and chest; it started to trickle down her temples. A vein throbbed in her neck whilst the odd tear leaked out to drop into the murky water in front of her.

When Annabel had finished hanging the shirt by the fire, she noticed a dark stain growing on the back of Hetty's current skirt. She was still bleeding and it looked bad.

"Patsy," Annabel whispered, trying not to sound alarmed. "Can you just have a look at something for me?" She motioned towards Hetty. Patsy inspected the poor girl, her eyes wild with alarm.

"Hetty sit back," she ordered.

"No." Her voice was strained beyond recognition. "Have to finish."

"Hetty, please!" Patsy's voice was thick with desperation. At the sound of it Hetty looked up. Her grey eyes were bloodshot and her hair was now stuck to her pale face. She looked as though she wanted to protest but was overcome by another peel of agony. Letting out a long, strained scream, she bent over her writhing bump, rocking slightly as if this movement would somehow stem the hurt. Suppressed tears now raced down her cheeks. Her face was soon saturated with them.

"Make it stop Patsy. Please make it stop."

"I'll try. I'll get help."

"No!" Hetty seized Patsy's arm, her knuckles white. "I don't think there's time. Tom – Tom'll make it worse."

Patsy obviously saw truth in these words and sat back down, stroking the hair off of Hetty's face almost frantically.

"It's okay," Patsy crooned as Hetty gasped in the smoky air. "Anna, come to where I am, hold her head so I can have a look at 'er."

Annabel did as instructed, taking a wet shirt from the water to press against Hetty's clammy forehead.

"We have to get her to a doctor," she announced.

"No, if we take her anywhere Tom'll kill us all."

"I'll go – I'll fetch the doctor."

"No, you can't. The closest doctor's in your town – it's too far away."

"We can't just leave her like this!"

"We have to try on our own. She was fine for the others and they were twins."

Despite her words, the fear in Patsy's face betrayed her.

"Get it out Patsy! It doesn't feel like the others. I want it out," Hetty cried, sounding terrified. Annabel quickly realised this wasn't how child birth was meant to go at all.

As Patsy lifted Hetty's skirt Hetty began to scream in renewed agony, wriggling on the ground. Annabel tried desperately to hold her as still as she could so Patsy could examine her.

"She's been in labour for hours. Damn it Hetty!" she cursed. "Why didn't you tell me?"

The screaming grew louder and more pained as Hetty's body grew heavier in Annabel's arms. Her strength and will were diminishing rapidly.

Lowering Hetty's head carefully to the floor, Annabel jumped up. Pouring some water from a jug on the table into a cup, she held it up to Hetty's cracked lips. Hetty drank in small sips, clenching her mouth around the rim of the cup to hold off another scream.

Just as Annabel lowered the empty cup, the heavy door swung open, banging back on its frame. The figure in the doorway had Annabel shrinking against the wall.

It was Tom, Hetty's husband and the younger of the two men who had attacked her. She prayed that seeing his wife in such agony he would help her but Annabel soon realised this was an absurd idea. When he spoke, his voice was full of menace. He swayed dangerously on his feet as he stood there, almost too drunk to move.

"Get up whore!" he bellowed.

Hetty jumped, crying out in pain. She bent forwards onto all fours with considerable effort, trying to rise to her feet but her legs and arms were too weak to lift her. Tom crouched down, his face only an inch from hers.

"GET UP!" he screamed, spit flying from his foul smelling mouth. Annabel saw tears running off of Hetty's nose in the same rhythm as the blood now dripping steadily from her skirts.

Patsy rushed to her side, holding her weight as she tried once more to stand.

"Tom she's sick, she's having your child. Please have mercy."

Tom turned his attention to his younger sister, slapping his palm across her cheek. Annabel shrank further into the wall, wanting to help but frozen in terror.

"Shut up," he growled. "Women have babies all the time, why did my wife have to be so WEAK!"

"It's not the same this time Tom, let her rest I beg you!"

He laughed, grabbing Hetty's shoulders and shoved her to the floor. Blood gushed from beneath her dress, soaking the floor. Annabel screamed, covering her face. Patsy knelt at Hetty's side, looking more desperate than ever. Tom bent down at the same time, flinging Patsy towards the wall where she fell against the water tub with a metallic clang. Gripping his wife's chin, he put his nose against hers.

"Clean your mess up and deliver me a son within the hour. If you haven't washed my clothes and served my dinner by the time I get back, I'll make you wish you'd never been born."

The sight of Hetty, her face set in pain, tears streaming down her cheeks, made something in Annabel snap. She slid the heavy water jug off the table next to her cowering form and rose to her feet. Drawing back the jug she smashed it hard into Tom's temple making him collapse to the ground. Patsy climbed indifferently over him to once again examine Hetty, whose legs were now curled at an odd angle beneath her body, her face paler than ever. As Annabel watched, Hetty's eyes rolled back into her head and she shook violently. Annabel seized the wet shirt once more, placing it back into position over Hetty's hot skin, holding down her shoulders as she tried to arch herself away from the pain.

"Come on Hetty," Patsy cried. "You have to try."

Annabel saw the tendons in Hetty's neck straining, until she thought they must snap clean in two, as she tried with all her might to deliver this child for her disgusting husband.

Patsy shook almost as much as Hetty. She was covered from head to toe in blood and wild with panic. Annabel's head snapped up as she saw another male figure filling the open doorway. She bent over Hetty in a protective stance but when she looked at him again Annabel noticed he looked nothing like Tom or his father. He was a tall man with a slim but strong frame. From the blonde hair that fell over his eyes, she knew this must be Daniel.

His eyes darted from Hetty's broken form to Patsy and finally to Tom, unconscious on the floor. Daniel checked his brother's pulse, if anything looking slightly disappointed when he found it, then scooped him up and carried him outside, closing the door behind him.

Hetty's body was growing weaker by the second. She had lost too much blood already and was still losing more. Daniel re-entered the room a couple of minutes later, his arms laden with roughly cut blankets. Hetty strained with every ounce of energy she had left, screaming louder than Annabel thought possible.

After what felt like hours, the baby finally slid into Patsy's waiting grasp. Daniel took the child from his sister, cradling its head in one large hand, staining his skin with blood. A beautiful high-pitched wail escaped from the infants purple lips. They all smiled in relief as Daniel wrapped it quickly in another blanket, gently rubbing its back with strong, sure hands that told of experience. Patsy sliced the cord with a kitchen knife and continued to tend to the mother. Hetty tried desperately to lift her head enough to see her child, yet no longer had the physical strength to do so. Daniel, noticing her struggle, held the baby against Hetty's chest so she could look upon its face for the first time. She smiled as if oblivious to her suffering and stroked a tender finger over the baby's tiny head.

"Beautiful," Hetty whispered, and then her head fell back with another groan.

Daniel snatched up the child in concern. Hetty's tremors quickly became more violent, her entire body shaking on the floor until she was unable to stay on her back. She thrashed from side to side, her eyes once more rolling into her head. A dark stream of blood trickled from the corner of her mouth as she bit down on her tongue and her body became rigid. Annabel leaned against Hetty, pinning her to the floor, holding her head tightly between her palms. Her heart hammered against her chest. She had no idea what she was doing. She looked around in a panic but Daniel had left the room with the baby.

Patsy was sat on the floor trembling almost as badly as Hetty, her arms slick with blood. Her bloody face was streaked with tears, so thick she appeared to be choking on them, as she watched Hetty's writhing body vacantly.

Annabel stayed on top of Hetty, knowing in the bottom of her heart there was nothing she could do but she had to keep trying...had to keep up the pretense she was trying to save the young woman's tragic life.

Eventually Hetty's fit subsided and her body lay unmoving on the ground. The only sound in the room was the quiet hiss of the dying embers on the fire. The strong smell of blood filled Annabel's nostrils as she gazed upon Hetty's lifeless face.

Hurried footsteps approached the house before Daniel burst back inside. His eyes instantly went to Hetty. Silently, without so much as breathing, he cupped the back of her head, placing two fingers against her throat. He squeezed his eyes shut, hanging his head as Patsy let out a loud, involuntary sob.

Lifting her own shaky hand, Annabel pulled down Hetty's eyelids. It was in that moment she saw just how young Hetty was.

"How – how old was she?" she whispered, her throat so dry it was hard to speak. Her voice sounded wrong in this sombre room. She felt more like an intruder than ever.

"Seventeen," Daniel answered, so quietly it was practically inaudible. His voice was so smooth it was almost musical.

Moving his hand from Hetty's head Daniel brushed the tips of his fingers lightly over her cheek. Another loud sob from Patsy made him look up and he crawled over to her, pulling her into his chest. She clung to his back as if he were a life raft in her deep ocean of pain. His stubble covered chin rested on his younger sister's head as he rocked her like a child. The sound of her tears touched Annabel so deeply she couldn't stand it. Getting shakily to her feet she crept towards the door. Leaving the two siblings to their shared grief she made her way back to the stable. She almost fell through the door she was so emotionally exhausted, yet she found Billy there, huddled in the corner with a small bundle cradled lovingly in his arms.

"Sad," he said.

"Yes," Annabel croaked. "Hetty has gone to heaven," she added after a short pause.

Billy seemed to not quite understand the concept of a person dying and he'd never really spoken to Hetty. However, he knew Patsy cared about her like family. He looked up at Annabel.

"Patsy sad?" he asked.

"Yes," Annabel repeated, "and baby." At this they both glanced down at the little pink infant, still covered in Hetty's drying blood.

"Dani bring baby. Billy look after it."

Annabel, tripping over her feet, sank to the floor beside him, leaning her head on Billy's large shoulder. He patted it before returning his hand to the back of the child. Looking down into the blankets Annabel traced a finger across the baby's soft head and down its cheek, managing a small smile. They remained like that for an immeasurable amount of time, looking on at the small baby asleep in Billy's loving arms.

Daniel and Patsy came in just as darkness was drawing in. Daniel had his arm around Patsy who was still sniffling, her eyes bright red and bloodshot. They came over, sitting around the baby as if in some nativity parody.

"What – what is it?" she hiccupped, motioning towards the baby. Annabel shook her head and looked towards Billy. When he didn't answer either she gently peered beneath the blankets.

"A girl."

Annabel heard Daniel suck in a breath through his teeth.

"He'll kill her," he stated.

"What do we do?"

"I don't know." Daniel ran a hand through his blonde hair, sweeping it out of his eyes. "'e can't know. We keep her 'ere. Say – say that Hetty and the baby both died - I put him outside, I'll tell 'im when he wakes up. Had he passed out from drink?"

"No," Patsy's voice sounded rough and strained. "'e was drunk alright, 'urtin' Hetty he was. Anna hit him. Good job too he woulda...well, I guess she died anyway didn't she?"

Daniel put his arm back around Patsy's shoulder as she sniffled and he looked up at Annabel. There was softness in his hazel eyes. They were the exact same shade as Billy's.

"Thank you," he whispered. A small crease appeared between his brows. "Let's hope he don't remember when he wakes." He gave her a small, tight smile.

"You're Daniel aren't you?"

The corners of his mouth twitched slightly and he nodded.

"This ain't how we shoulda met. Shouldn't of met at all really. I'm sorry you were brought here."

There was hell in his eyes too, that haggard look of seeing too much too young. He kissed the top of Patsy's head in a fatherly way before moving to stand up. She clung onto him.

"I need to move Hetty. Mama'll be back soon and you know she's on their side. She can't know before Tom. I'll be right back, promise."

Patsy nodded, letting her hands fall limply at her sides. "We'll bury her soon."

Daniel squeezed Patsy's shoulder. "It's the least she deserves."

He stood up, making his way to the door. They all knew they couldn't leave Hetty alone in that house.

"The baby needs to go up the ladder," Patsy whispered. "She can't be found."

"No. Baby no leave." Billy clung to the baby tighter.

"No Billy, baby's not goin' away. Just moving her upstairs, it'll be safer. Tom won't get her up there."

"Horses be lonely."

"No they've got each other, baby's got no one."

"Baby got Billy." He kissed her small head. "Billy baby's papa now."

Nobody had ever, in the history of man, uttered anything with more determination than Billy just then. As the words hung in the silent air the four of them drank them in, nourished by a new, fleeting sense of hope.

Patsy stood up, explaining that she needed to find milk for the now restless baby. Annabel thought Patsy also wanted to be alone, to have time to think over the horrific events of the day without anyone watching her, so she let her go without protest.

The baby, hungry and exhausted after its stressful birth, began to whine and fidget in Billy's cradling arms. He jiggled her up and down but this just made it worse. Holding her tighter to him they both sat in silent terror, listening for footfalls outside the door. In their fright they convinced each other that every breath of wind was a voice, every stomp of the horse's hooves was a fist falling onto supple flesh.

Both Billy and Annabel jumped almost out of their own skin when Patsy threw open the door, her arms laden with buckets of water and milk. The baby sucked on this sustenance greedily as Billy dripped it into her mouth. Patsy had clearly washed herself in the stream as well when she had fetched the water. Her face and arms were now clean, although her dress was still splattered with blood. Annabel slurped the water out of her cupped hands, feeling the cool liquid radiate through her body.

When Daniel re-emerged a few minutes later, his face was lined with new sadness. His own skin had been washed in the stream as well.

Now they were all together, they ascended into the loft. Annabel and Patsy went first. Her legs still shaky from shock Annabel slipped on the first rung, falling back down to the floor. Daniel placed a hand on her arm to steady her. Annabel started. The touch was familiar, safe. She turned her attentions back to the ladder as she tried to remember where she could have met him before, her mind came up blank.

Daniel followed behind Annabel, carrying a water

bucket in one hand, climbing with the other. Billy was also adept at climbing this ladder, so was able to carry the baby at the same time. When they reached the top, Billy washed the child in the water, leaving a tender hand behind her head as he did so. Slowly, as the blood and mucus peeled away, they saw the beautiful pink skin of the baby and the soft tufts of dark brown hair atop her delicate head. When her eyes opened for the first time they were the exact same, stunning grey of Hetty's. As if they had been carved from solid crystal.

Billy, with a gentle, caring touch, managed to rock the child to sleep almost instantly, drifting off himself moments later. As they watched Billy and the baby sleeping peacefully in the corner, Daniel ran his hands through his hair looking defeated. He drew in a shaky breath.

"I – I told Tom wha' happened. He woke up an' saw me on me way back. I said Hetty hadn't survived. I told him the baby was a girl but that she died with Hetty. He's angry more than sad. Hit me, saying she was too weak and deserved to die. But 'e's too drunk to get me proper now. Said he already had two sons, she'd done 'er duty."

Tears were leaking out of Annabel's eyes, she swiped them away, annoyed at her own emotions. She had been here five minutes. These wonderful, brave people had been here their entire lives. Daniel reached a hand across to hers, squeezing her fingers awkwardly. They both sat stock still, frightened by this rare form of physical and emotional closeness. Slowly he reached out his other arm and placed it back around Patsy's shoulders, securing a bond between the three of them that would last their entire lives.

Chapter Nine

When it was deemed late enough to be safe, Daniel snuck into the house next door, coveting a large bowl of the burnt stew Patsy and her mother had cooked. Saving some for Billy, the three allies ate with only the sound of their chewing to fill the heavy darkness.

Daniel's eyes were fixed on Annabel as she greedily lapped up the last of her stew.

"You need more food," he muttered, in an attempt to lighten the mood somewhat but he wasn't really into it. His voice sounded as lifeless as his smile. "I can find you more if you like."

"No, really it's alright," she insisted. "I'm just being greedy. Don't go out of your way. Stay here where it's safe."

"I'll bring you a candle in the morning," Patsy said, almost as if un-aware the others had spoken at all. She stood up. Daniel watched her with the same concerned crease between his brows. She walked to the makeshift bed where she curled up, facing the wall.

"Anna," she murmured.

Hearing the despair in her friend's voice Annabel sat

beside her.

"What is it?"

"Tell me something 'bout your manor. Tell me 'bout the jewels again, so I don' dream about today."

"Of course."

Brushing a strand of fiery hair off of Patsy's face, as a mother might do to their child, Annabel once more began to describe her former fairy tale life, as if she were reading a bedtime story. A single tear fled from her eye as she spoke, realising with a heavy heart how pointless everything in that life had been. The dresses, the jewels, the etiquette and standards had all been nothing but a ridiculous show of her own self-perceived importance.

Patsy's hand stroked over a square of cow hide as Annabel spoke, looking more childlike than ever. After a while her shoulders began to shake.

Leaving Patsy to her grief, Annabel kissed her cheek before settling back beside Daniel. At some point in her tale he had retreated back down the ladder to fetch more hay which he had arranged on the floor. After easing the baby from Billy's slack arms he placed her into something resembling a nest. Billy curled up beside her as if on instinct, still snoring quietly.

"I'm sorry," Annabel whispered. She knew this was an empty thing to say even before the words had formed on her lips.

"For what?" Daniel asked.

"Hetty. I should have done more. I don't know what, but surely there was something -"

"There was nothin', you did better than anyone else could 'ave."

"But it wasn't enough."

A long silence followed these words. The desperate sadness pounded through her blood until Annabel could barely stand it. She wanted to wake up, to go back to her fine things...for an imperfect cup of tea to be her biggest worry.

After all they had witnessed, Daniel and Annabel were unaware of anything left to say. Every topic seemed so trivial. Besides, Annabel didn't know anything about Daniel, nor him about her. The tension grew until out of nowhere, Daniel started to hum.

He chose a melancholy tune, his forearms resting against his knees and his head bent towards the ground, as if in prayer. Annabel had never heard the song before but it fit the situation so perfectly she could have cried. Her ears prickled and strained as she listened with rapt attention. It was the most beautiful sound she had ever heard. His voice carried the song perfectly, staying low and quiet yet smooth, gliding over the notes with practiced ease. She brought her own knees up under her chin and tilted her head to the side, shuffling subconsciously closer. She truly believed in that moment, she would do anything for the people in that small, grimy stable. The realisation was at the same time both terrifying and exhilarating.

All too soon Daniel stopped singing. The darkness mourned the loss of his music, once more becoming thick and oppressive. It crept into every crevice of the small room so Annabel felt blind, unable to even see her hands three inches from her face.

Hearing Daniel shift beside her she looked up. She only saw the whites of his eyes facing her in the gloom. The sounds of Patsy's grief had drifted some time ago into the uneven breath of someone deep in slumber. Every now and then a groan escaped her lips and Annabel felt sure she was reliving the horrific birth of the baby as she slept.

"What happened to Hetty?" Annabel asked, speaking quietly to avoid disturbing her sleeping friends. Daniel didn't answer for a few minutes but when he did his voice sounded strained, as if he too were anxious. He seemed on the surface to be dealing with Hetty's horrible death with an almost blasé attitude but, having been at the scene herself, Annabel saw that deep down he was barely clinging on.

"I don't know," he whispered. He sounded angry. "Tom took her. I didn't wanna tell Patsy, it'd make 'er worse."

He shuffled, unable to sit still at the mention of his brother. Annabel's cheeks grew hot with anger as well.

"What will he do to her?"

Daniel's arm brushed Annabel's as he ran a hand through his hair, drawing in another shaky breath.

"I – I don't know." His voice caught and his body stiffened. His shoulder next to hers was trembling, making the material of her dress scratch against her skin. She didn't dare move.

"She deserved more – so much more. I shoulda given it to 'er. She wanted me but I - I thought she'd marry someone better, someone good for her. I got angry when she had the twins, didn't understand why she'd done it. I thought she were gettin' back at me for - for breakin' her heart. I left her alone 'cuz Tom was already jealous, thought we were sleepin' together or summit but I never, not with her. I didn't see her like that. I shoulda helped her more. I shoulda been there...or married 'er when she asked, not put her in 'is way."

"You didn't Daniel. How could you have known this would happen?"

"She was always fiery. She wanted what she wanted ya know? But I jus'...there was another girl I liked, but then tha' didn't work. She were havin' it away with another man, ran off to the town with 'im. I had to stay 'ere, had to keep an eye on Hetty. Seein' Hetty with Tom, weak an' broken after I'd turned her down for someone worth less than nothin' to me now. It nearly killed me every day."

"Did you love Hetty?"

There was another long silence.

"Not the way she wanted, as a friend or a sister perhaps, but nothin' more. I coulda looked after 'er though... helped her. Maybe I coulda got her outta this shit heap."

"You can't blame yourself Daniel. You just can't. It wasn't your fault. You will go mad convincing yourself that it was."

"Then why do I feel like this?" His voice caught and his shoulder shook even more. Letting go of her reservations Annabel stretched out her hand and folded it around his.

It was rough beneath her touch but all the more comforting for its imperfection.

"Because you cared and that is never ever something to let go of."

It was then, with the comforting touch of another human being beside him, that he let go completely. Finally unable to keep the tears from pouring out of his eyes they dripped down onto the dust carpeted floor with a soft, rhythmic plunk. Annabel moved her hand tentatively onto his broad back, rubbing it in some feeble attempt to comfort him.

His shirt was warm beneath her palm. The sound of his emotion, so close to her ear, stirred feelings deep within Annabel's heart. She wanted to cry along with him but she held back. These people had seen hell; she didn't have the right to cry.

Slowly, Daniel's breathing evened out and Annabel let him go, allowing him to wipe his eyes roughly with the heels of his hands and brush the hair once more from his face. He leaned back against the wall. Annabel's hands felt empty now as they rested in her lap. Daniel seemed to notice Annabel's loneliness and put his hand back in hers. She leaned her head against the wall too. Daniel began to hum again, the same melancholy tune. Annabel felt his body vibrate with the sound, as the music completely filled her every sense. She closed her eyes against the oppressive darkness and drifted slowly into a dreamless sleep, the reassuring warmth of Daniel at her side.

They all slept fitfully that night, being woken at least

every hour by the shrill shrieks of the tiny baby in their midst, calling out for the mother who would never come. The cries seemed to convey pain from her very soul.

However, when Annabel awoke in the morning, she felt oddly warm. Becoming aware of the body beside her almost immediately, she opened her eyes.

They had shifted in their unconsciousness so Annabel's head was now resting on Daniel's shoulder. She pressed herself closer to him, still half asleep as she listened to the rhythm of his heart. He smelt of soap and earth...a smell that once again Annabel found strangely familiar, although her foggy brain couldn't conjure up the appropriate memory. A few moments later Daniel began to stir as well, jerking awake and letting go of Annabel as if he'd been burned. He stood up quickly, looking down as hurt crossed over Annabel's face, followed by the shock that she had been so close to someone for such an extended period of time.

Daniel looked as if he wanted to say something. Seeming to change his mind at the last minute, he turned and bent down to check on Patsy, still asleep on the straw. He touched her shoulder lightly, stirring her from sleep. When she opened her eyes they were red and puffy, as if she had been crying all night. Her face was blotchy whilst her chestnut hair stuck up in strange angles. The worst thing about her was a frightening vacancy in the depths of her dark eyes...there had always been so much passion about her. Daniel was talking now in a low, sympathetic voice, his hand still resting on Patsy's shoulder whilst she nodded at various intervals in the conversation.

Annabel was still sat in the same spot, stiff and achy from another night of sleeping on the floor, her more prominent bones having rubbed against the hard wood. It felt like new bruises were blooming up already.

Quietly both Patsy and Daniel rose. As Patsy walked past, she brushed a hand over the top of Annabel's head. Daniel supported Patsy's clumsy steps as they climbed down the ladder, whilst simultaneously avoiding Annabel's gaze with a slightly worried frown, almost identical to the one currently creasing Patsy's forehead. A few more seconds passed before the thud of the door closing resonated through the stable. The sound jerked Billy awake. His eyes darted immediately towards the sleeping infant in concern. The baby was already awake but for once was silent, kicking out her tiny legs with small, jerky movements.

"Morning Billy," Annabel croaked, wincing as a sharp pain shot down her neck when she tried to stretch it. She massaged the muscles, loosening the crick and thought longingly of the feather pillows back in the manor. Billy had now gathered the baby into his arms and was rocking her slowly. He glanced at Annabel and grinned, revealing all of his small, brown teeth.

"Mornin' Anna." He looked back down at the child. "Baby happy," he stated.

Still on his knees, Billy shuffled towards Annabel, coating his thin trousers with dust. When he reached her he shifted the baby wordlessly into her arms.

"Billy go." He inclined his head towards the door and she understood that he must work. She cradled the baby closer to her chest. It was the first time she had ever held a baby before. The weight felt strange in her arms.

Watching the baby's eyes roaming in their sockets, desperately trying to figure out the world around her, Annabel felt saddened that Hetty would never be able to look upon these tiny features. Never be able to smile at how perfect they were. Never be able to hear the soft breath entering and leaving the newly formed lungs, or to marvel at the complexities of every little thing about her youngest child. A single tear fled down Annabel's cheek, landing on the baby's forehead. She watched it trickle down into the soft tuft of raven hair before wiping it gently away.

Annabel now felt a much more familiar feeling stir in her breast...anger. How could this child grow up without a mother? Death was always described in the bible as something beautiful, glorious.

Hetty's had been anything but.

She hoped beyond anything there was something like heaven for Hetty to escape her pain, yet in her heart of hearts she knew there wasn't. Hetty would rot in the ground, or whatever godforsaken place Tom had dumped her and become nothing more than food for the worms. There wasn't anything poetic about that.

Chapter Ten

When Billy returned, he looked down at the baby suckling on the tip of Annabel's finger, just as she let out a little cry of hunger.

"Baby happy?" he questioned, sitting down heavily.

"Yes," Annabel replied. "Yes she is."

"What baby name?" Billy asked, looking at Annabel quizzically. This was something Annabel hadn't even considered. It seemed absurd now, that a child should remain nameless.

"Oh...um...Hetty didn't...let's wait for Daniel and Patsy. Then we will come up with one together."

Billy nodded so excitedly it looked as if his head would fly off. Annabel let out a little laugh, feeling warmth radiate through her at the mere sight of him. Annabel racked her brains for a suitable name, looking down at the baby in her arms every time she thought of one, to see if it fit the small face looking back at her.

Daniel returned around lunch time, bounding up the ladder with ease and agility. He had a jug of milk clasped in one hand.

"Patsy's with Mama, makin' food I think."

Diamonds Fall

He strolled over to Annabel and Billy's huddle, plopping down beside them and directing his gaze to the baby.

"Does your mother know about Hetty?" Annabel asked. "Was she ever so upset?"

To Annabel's surprise Daniel snorted in amusement, "was she 'ell. Jus' one less mouth t' feed innit?"

Annabel took in a sharp breath. It made a hissing noise as it passed her teeth.

"She had her emotion beat outta her years ago Anna. No need'a be shocked. It's just life here."

There was nothing to say to such a comment so they reverted back to silence, until Patsy's wild hair appeared at the top of the ladder. She was so quiet nobody even heard her enter the stable. With her came the smell of fresh bread. Annabel's mouth began to water in anticipation as Patsy tore up the misshapen loaf and gave a piece to everyone. It was still warm. Annabel held it between her cold hands for a few seconds, eating as slowly as she could to savour the feeling of the food sliding down into her stomach, the flavours filling her mouth.

When she had finished Billy thrust the fresh milk into Annabel's hands, giving her a not so subtle hint that the baby should be fed as well. As the baby drank with loud, desperate sucking noises, Annabel faced the group.

"Billy mentioned we should name the baby. I think he is right. Do you know whether Hetty had a name planned?"

"George," Patsy replied humorously. "No point thinkin' about a girl's name."

She cast her eyes down to the floor again, fidgeting

with a piece of hair that had fallen in front of her face.

"Um...well, I have been thinking all day and I want to ask your opinion...because she is, of course, your niece but there was some member of royalty who I once met in France called Genevieve. She had the same pale eyes as the baby does, so I thought...maybe Genevieve would work. It's not too dissimilar to George...I mean, it still begins with a G." Annabel broke off, looking around at the others faces, trying to gage their reactions. Patsy simply nodded.

"What little girl don't wanna be a princess, eh? Genevieve, yeah it works." Daniel replied, smiling.

Billy looked on frowning, his mouth moving as if he were trying to figure out exactly how to place the name on his tongue.

"Jen!" he shouted out triumphantly as he came up with the abbreviation. Annabel winced, about to dissuade him from such a shortening but Patsy nodded again.

"Jen," she muttered, smiling to herself, "yeah, she's Jen."

Seeing the joy that filled all of the faces around her, Annabel just let herself be carried along with their merriment.

"Hello Jen," Billy repeated the name, smiling down at Genevieve.

A sudden thought struck Annabel...that Billy might accidentally mention the baby when he was out on his chores, without knowing the danger he would be putting her in.

"Billy," she said, looking intently into his eyes. "I have to tell you something, okay?"

He nodded, excited by the look on Annabel's face.

"You must not tell anyone about Jen, alright?"

He nodded.

"No one, not Papa, not Mama, not Tom. Especially not Tom, you understand?"

"Yes," he said with determination. "She is secret. Billy keep secret."

Annabel let out a sigh of relief, smiling up at Billy who grinned back. He, of all people, understood the cruelty that could be unleashed by his family, if they found Genevieve. Annabel transferred the baby into Billy's waiting arms as Daniel ruffled his hair, making him laugh.

"Genevieve Henrietta Prince." Patsy muttered from where she was leaning against the wall besides Daniel.

"Your surname's Prince?" Annabel asked.

"Not what you expected, huh?" Daniel laughed.

"Well...I - I never knew. That makes her name even more perfect."

They sat absorbing the small sounds and movements of the newly named Genevieve Prince, until Daniel and Patsy's names could be heard being hollered from next door. Daniel groaned and got to his feet, making his way down the ladder with just a small, reluctant wave. Patsy blew a kiss as she descended after him.

The rest of the day passed in a daze, filled with Genevieve's cries and a frantic rush to silence them. Billy was astoundingly adept at taking care of a baby, noticing her distress often before she made a sound. So much love exuded from him that any worries Annabel may have had for Genevieve's wellbeing dispersed immediately.

As night was creeping in, Patsy came back into the stable, dripping wet from the torrential rain now pounding against the thin wooden roof. In her hands were several of the candles she had promised just the night before.

"Daniel's hunting," she muttered, her teeth chattering slightly.

"Seriously? He will catch his death."

"Nah, 'e's fine. You rather go 'ungry?"

In reply Annabel's stomach let out a loud growl and they both laughed. The laughter however, was thin and lasted only a couple of seconds. Annabel never went out in the rain; she didn't really know what rain felt like.

To cover her embarrassment, Annabel busied herself positioning the candles around them, hoping they would produce some sort of heat if ever she could figure out how to light them. She didn't think they would possess a match.

Patsy walked over to Billy and Genevieve sat in the corner. Looking into the small face of her niece she said almost inaudibly, "shall we baptise her?"

"What?" Annabel replied, unsure whether she had heard correctly.

"She's so little. I've seen babies die without bein' baptized an' knowin' they can't get to heaven...I know it won' be proper, bu' God must...I dunno, please?" Annabel was skeptical and worried that Patsy was already anticipating this infant's death. However, having seen what little of this family she had, she agreed.

"Do you want to wait for Daniel?" Annabel asked.

Patsy shook her head. "No, 'e thinks I'm mad believin' in heaven."

Annabel nodded again, silently agreeing more with Daniel's point of view. How could someone live here and still believe in heaven? Where would someone even learn about heaven here? Patsy looked at Annabel expectantly.

"Wha' do we 'ave to do?" Patsy prompted.

"Oh, right. Well I think we should...light the candles and then..."

Annabel looked around her for inspiration, running a hand across her eyes as she tried to think back to the christenings she had attended. She had always been too consumed in the way the other guests were admiring her dress, whilst running her own eyes over everyone else's less flattering attire, to pay much attention to the service itself.

"And holy water, I think that is quite important."

There was a pause as Patsy lit the candles and looked at Annabel confused, unsure how to acquire the second request.

"Oh...um...normal water should be fine. Yes, just normal water."

Patsy scurried from the room, returning only a matter of minutes later with the water.

"I've never prayed before, do you think God will mind?" Patsy asked sheepishly as she knelt beside the water, watching as it settled in the bucket.

"No, he will forgive you in a heartbeat," Annabel replied, gesturing to Billy to follow her over to the bucket too.

Once they were all knelt in a circle, she took both Billy and Patsy's hands and began a prayer above the water. They asked forgiveness for their sins and impurity. They spoke of the pure heart of the baby and asked for her to have health, intelligence and a good life. Following this Annabel took up the baby and held her above the water. Genevieve wriggled and kicked out her legs in anticipation. Splashing water over the baby's head, Annabel recited the Lord's Prayer, the only prayer she had bothered to remember off the top of her head. As she reached the end of the prayer she drew a cross with her fingers on Genevieve's forehead. She was making it up but she wanted it to as least sound convincing. To her own ears her words sounded empty and ridiculous but Patsy and Billy both watched with rapt attention.

"Genevieve Henrietta Prince, I offer you to God as a servant to our Lord. I, Annabel Maria Hoddington, hereby swear to protect her from all earthly harm and to submit this child, your daughter, to your care when you deem the moment right. Do you, Patricia and William Prince, swear in the name of God, to do the same?"

"Yes," they chanted in unison.

Annabel bent down and kissed Genevieve on the head. Picking up a blanket she then wrapped her tightly back inside it.

"All done," Annabel smiled.

Patsy had taken the child in her own arms and now held her tightly - as if her life depended on it - rocking her to soothe her gentle cries. Anxious at the sound, Billy scooped her up, away from his younger sister, calming the infant almost at once.

It was a lovely sight to see Billy and Patsy cooing around the baby sandwiched between them. They had the same round faces, their mouths curving upwards in the exact same way. Annabel stood and watched their sibling chemistry for a while, drinking in their stolen moment. Annabel knew then, even with the trauma already tainting her tiny life, Genevieve would never live without love.

Chapter Eleven

Having completed Genevieve's christening, it dawned in everyone's mind just how unfair it would be not to fight for a funeral to be held for Hetty. Patsy and Annabel, the guilt still gnawing at their innards, both agreed it was the least they could do, having been unable to save Hetty in the first place. Billy took Genevieve, he still did not quite understand the fate that had befallen Hetty and Patsy was anxious to keep it that way. As they left the stable, Patsy held onto Annabel's arm for reassurance, as well as to show anybody who may be peeking out of their houses that she was in control of Annabel, not her ally...a necessity to avoid more abuse befalling them both. The feeling of constantly being watched still held that same threatening, sinister quality. They both knew that should they take a single step in the wrong direction, they would be hunted down immediately.

Annabel was sure everyone had heard about Hetty by now, many of whom would have heard the screaming first hand yet stood in their houses, too cowardly to help.

Patsy told Annabel of how Tom had confronted both her and Daniel together, accusing them of spiting him by stealing his child. He didn't even mention the loss of his wife. He demanded to see Jen simply to take her down to the stream and drown her. He was convinced Hetty had to have been unfaithful. He believed himself not weak enough to produce females. For a brief, terrifying moment, he had accused Daniel of fathering the child, yet seemed to deem this idea ludicrous after a few moments.

Finishing her recollection, Patsy led Annabel into the dimly lit house next to the stable to find Patsy's mother, once more crouched by the fire stirring a thin stew.

"Mama," Patsy greeted, bending down to kiss the older woman on her cheek. She did not even look up. A dark bruise was shadowing the cheek closest to the fire.

"You ruined the stew yesterday Pat and then you wasted it on her."

Patsy looked stung.

"Mama I was...Hetty was..." She was unable to finish that sentence. "She needed me Mama."

"I needed you Pat. You know your father doesn't like waiting and the mess she made."

"You can't be that cold Mama, Hetty's..." she took a shuddering breath. "Where is she Mama, where did they take her?"

Patsy hadn't been fooled by Daniel's white lie. She knew Tom had taken her. Patsy's mother closed her eyes for a moment, as if weary to her very bones.

"I don't know Patsy," she sighed.

"Yes you do." Patsy's voice had turned as hard as ice. "Tell me where she is. I gotta give 'er somethin' as a funeral, please Mama."

Her mother simply stirred the stew with the same slow turns, her eyes fixed on the ripples the ladle made in the watery mixture.

"She migh' be jus' in the trees. I dunno where they took 'er but I saw 'em carry 'er in the forest last night. She won' be on the path, they're clever." She said this with a sickening amount of pride in her voice.

"Thank you Mama," Patsy whispered, grasping Annabel's elbow again and steering her outside into the rain.

They found Hetty's body more by smell than sight. She was still covered in blood and almost blue in colour. There was already evidence of where insects and forest animals had taken their sustenance from her flesh. Turning away, Annabel threw up in a bush directly behind her, emptying her stomach completely until she was just dry heaving onto the leaves.

"We - we need to find Daniel," Patsy said, stronger in stomach than Annabel but still appalled and sickened. Something in Patsy's face suggested this wasn't the first time she had seen a corpse. Carefully untying Hetty's blood stained apron, Patsy draped it over her unseeing face, affording Hetty this one last shred of dignity.

Annabel heard someone approaching, twigs were snapping beneath heavy boots. However, these footfalls were steady and light. Turning around Annabel saw Daniel walking towards her with long, focused strides, as if he were concentrating really hard on this simple action. That way he could avoid the sight of Hetty on the saturated ground. Still lost in her own shock and grief, Patsy fell to her knees and began to scoop the wet mud into her hands, making a small hole in the ground. She dumped handfuls of mud beside her. Dirt coated her dress and arms in seconds. Annabel, realising that Patsy was trying to dig a grave, quickly joined her in the chore. It was absurd, Annabel knew that and so did Patsy, but still they continued.

Sighing, out of weariness as opposed to impatience, Daniel laid a hand gently on his sister's shoulder and pulled her back until she was resting on her heels.

"I'll go get a spade."

Annabel breathed out in relief. Her tender hands were already scratched and raw from only a few seconds of the work. She sat back as well, watching Daniel's form retreat into the trees. He returned a few moments later with only one spade and a loaf of slightly burnt bread, which he threw at the women before sliding the metal tool into the ground with a swift, efficient movement. The sound of the spade slicing through the earth was akin to a sword, Annabel thought, as she nibbled on the bread absentmindedly. Patsy jumped up to help Daniel, not even touching her own bread, but he picked her up and plonked her back down like a toddler. With a loud groan, sounding almost like a growl, Patsy crossed her arms over her chest and squinted in Daniel's direction, watching the pile of mud increase in size beside the deepening grave. Tears were once more falling silently down her cheeks, gouging tracks through the dirt that had somehow found a way onto her face and mixing with the cold, steady rain water that sent a chill down Annabel's spine.

When the grave was finally finished, Daniel climbed out and flopped down beside them, exhausted. His hands were bloodied and blistered, whilst all of their clothes were sodden from the rain and caked in mud. Patsy stood up slowly and cradled Hetty in her arms. Despite the putrid smell her body gave off, she lowered her into the grave, careful not to move the apron away from her deformed face.

"I - I think we should say summit," Patsy croaked. The others nodded their affirmation and she continued. "He-Hetty, thank you for givin' up everythin' to be part of our family, even if you were only with us f-for a little bit, it were really nice. I'm gunna miss you and I promise to look after your little g-g-girl and to show her how much she is loved, every single day."

Tears ran down all of their faces as they threw a handful of dirt into the grave and Daniel picked up his shovel again, wiping sweat from his already sodden brow. At the exact moment the shovel sliced back into the earth, a great flash of lightning illuminated the sky and a peel of thunder rolled over the tree tops. Annabel watched in silence, the rain plastering her hair to her face and making her shiver even more violently.

When the earth had been replaced, forming a mound above Hetty's body, Annabel once more repeated the Lord's Prayer and Patsy laid two branches on the ground to form a cross.

The three mourners turned to walk the few feet onwards, towards the grey stream where they each plunged their heads in and drank until they were full, lowering their aching bodies, fully clothed into the icy river, to rid themselves of the ghastly remnants of Hetty's tomb.

Dripping wet but clean, they headed back to the stable.

Once inside they immediately climbed up into the loft and sat on Annabel's bed, as close together as they could manage to get, feeding off of each other's body warmth in the hope of getting dry. They were tired beyond belief, hardly able to move a single muscle. Daniel's hands were cut up and bleeding, his shirt sleeves spotted with blood where he had touched them. Annabel glanced down at her own hands, noticing how much rougher they looked than they used to.

It took both Patsy and Annabel to lift the ladder that evening, they both refused to let Daniel so much as stand up. Once they were sat on Annabel's bed, they would not have moved if the entire stable had burst into flames...in fact, they would have been glad for the warmth the inferno would have provided.

Billy and Genevieve were both sleeping peacefully when they returned. Their eyes roamed behind their closed lids as they got lost in their own individual dreams. For that, at least, the three friends were glad.

Sitting on Annabel's bed, watching the two dreamers, they each felt some sort of peace that they had given Hetty something of a burial. That they had granted some sort of dignity to her gruesome demise.

Finally able to rest after the physically and emotionally exhausting day Annabel smiled, resting her head back against the straw. The bed was so narrow that all three of them had to lie incredibly close. At first Annabel stiffened, having been brought up to shun all kinds of touch. However, Daniel and Patsy's warmth was irresistible and once her teeth had finally stopped chattering, she quickly relaxed, drifting off into a restful sleep, lulled by Daniel's gentle humming beside her.

She thought she would never be able to sleep on her own again now she knew what it meant to sleep next to someone. Daniel's heartbeat, so close to her skin, sent a strange thrill through her blood that she didn't understand. She woke up a few hours later something close to content, having slept on a surface that seemed not to have created any new bruises.

The wind howled outside while the rain once more pounded on the roof. Daniel left at some point during the day to go about his daily chores, not willing to risk his family's wrath should he slack in his duties when everyone was already on the edge.

Patsy and Annabel passed the time easily, in constant conversation. Patsy fired endless questions at Annabel regarding her upbringing, still in awe of every detail, often asking for the same tales to be repeated multiple times. She asked about everything...the servants, the horses, the rooms in her house, even about Annabel's normal routines.

"How'd ya curl your hair? Why's it no' curly now?" Patsy asked, interrupting Annabel who was explaining her elaborate evening ritual.

"Put it in rags, don't you do that?"

"What? No!"

"I'll show you."

Sliding out from under the blanket, groaning as her stiff muscles complained at the movement, Annabel sliced the bottom few inches off of her moth eaten nightgown, with a knife Daniel had produced a few hours earlier from his boot. She shredded the fabric into thin strips before placing herself behind Patsy. Taking up a small section of hair she wrapped it tightly around a piece of the battered material, tying it into place at Patsy's scalp. She was unsure whether it would work on Patsy's frizzy strands but she was enjoying the process none the less.

"Of course, the rags I used weren't rags at all, they were custom made from velvet but the principle is the same." Annabel worked in silence for a while, her cheeks hot at how thoughtless that previous statement had been. "There you are...I think I've done it right. I'm not sure because a maid usually does it for me. Leave them in until the morning and we'll see if it's worked."

It was as she was performing this familiar task that Annabel realised just how little she had actually done for herself back at home. This almost felt like a merging of her former and present self, whilst being a mere shadow of them both. Once Annabel had finished wrapping Patsy's hair, Patsy jumped up. Ripping some of her own apron, she insisted on doing the same thing to Annabel's hair.

Daniel reappeared just as Patsy took up the first section

of Annabel's hair; he laughed at the sight. "I'd be in for it if Papa saw me hanging 'round with girls, doing hair no less."

Yet he stayed sat at the end of the bed, humming softly, a slight sparkle in his eyes. Whilst Patsy fiddled with Annabel's hair, raveling and unravelling it again as she made mistakes, Annabel took her first proper look at Daniel. He was stretched out with his ankles crossed, leaning against the wall. His hands were clasped behind his head in a picture of ease. His skin was slightly tanned. Freckles dotted his wonky nose in a way that Annabel thought entirely pleasant, although knowing he was the exact opposite to what she was supposed to find beautiful. She couldn't understand why she had been so afraid of freckles before, they added so much character to a person's skin.

Unlike the men Annabel had seen at the various functions in high society, Daniel had thin lines between his eyes and his sinewy muscles were more defined from a lifetime of hard work.

Perhaps the most pleasant thing about Daniel was that he looked nothing like his father or Tom, instead sharing his blonde hair and hazel eyes with Billy.

After a while Daniel's humming turned quieter and eventually stopped as his breathing regulated, betraying the fact he had drifted off to sleep. He looked incredibly peaceful. The lines had relaxed on his head, showing his face in a more youthful light...he was, after all, only a year or so older than Annabel. Patsy must have seen the direction of Annabel's gaze. She finished securing the last rag in her hair. It felt a lot looser than when her maids did it.

"D'ya have a man waitin' for you at 'ome?" Patsy asked. An image of the giant ring Annabel had locked in her armoire filled her mind.

"Yes, a fiancé."

"You're getting' married?" Patsy sounded incredulous.

"I think so, if he still wants to." Annabel doubted that anyone would want to marry her now, especially not the most eligible bachelor in the country. He would have women falling at his feet. No doubt he was already engaged or married to someone else by now. Their engagement had not even been announced, it had only ever been rumour.

"Is he good lookin'?"

"So I'm told."

"You mean you never even met 'im?"

"No that's not really how it works. It's more...a transaction. Father spoke to his father and they mutually agreed that our union will be good, for the advancement of both families. He's the richest man in the entire country and I was the richest woman." She shrugged, feeling as if she needed to justify herself.

"Oh, so that's what betrothed means! You mentioned it by the stream tha' first time, but I wasn't sure. Anyway, I know I dunno a lot 'bout marriage but ain't it good to love 'em first?"

"That is all good for the first year at most but when the love fades, you're left powerless and impoverished. Love is a good fairytale to tell little girls, it is not reality. Marrying Theodore Brogan will be best for my future."

"I don' think I'll ever get married," Patsy muttered almost inaudibly. Annabel was shocked, everyone got married, it was just how things were done.

"What? Never?"

"If love's jus' a story, why would I? I've never seen it end happily, so why'd I wanna make myself miserable?" Annabel laughed at this.

"You're so melancholy, of course you'll marry, you must!" Patsy looked a little angry at this presumption so Annabel adopted a more tender expression and tried again. "Not all men are like your father Patsy, when you leave here you will understand."

The younger girl just nodded. "I'll leave soon as the boys are big enough to come with me."

"What boys?"

"Hetty's boys! Tom takes 'em with him everywhere, they don' stand a chance. I gotta take 'em with me. It's why I've stayed so long...that an' until you came, I never knew a better world existed."

Annabel felt a strange mixture of emotions; she was both sad and happy at the same time. She had made a difference in a positive way to someone's life and it felt exhilarating, yet she didn't hold the power to truly do anything about it.

"I gotta take Billy wi' me too," Patsy continued. "And Jen and Daniel...none of them belong here either. Now Hetty's gone there ain't nothin' to stay for once I got 'er boys. We gotta wait for the right moment."

"It will come soon Patsy, I promise. And when it does I will help you in every way I can."

She let this new information sink in, wrapping a consoling arm around Patsy's shoulder. She was going home, although when still remained unknown. It could be years for all she knew and she could still end up prey to Tom and Trevor's anger or desire before then.

The door downstairs flew open, banging against the wall. The sound reverberated around the stable. Both Patsy and Annabel stiffened, Daniel stirred in his sleep. After several moments of silence, filled only with the howling of the bitter wind, Patsy peeked downstairs.

"It was just the wind."

Annabel sighed in relief. The dread it had been Tom or Trevor subsided and she relaxed against the straw. In his sleep Daniel wrapped a protective arm around her waist. Annabel flinched at first, sour memories flooded back into her mind and her heart rate sped up dramatically. However the warmth of Daniel's arm seeped through to her skin and she began to drift slowly off into sleep beside him.

Chapter Twelve

The wind continued to howl well into the night, the door banging open so often they eventually just left it to swing on its hinges. The thuds of it bashing against the wall startled them awake every few minutes. Genevieve's cries, mixed with the ferocious weather, left any hope of sleep nothing more than a distant day dream.

Just before dawn, when the wind had died down to a low whistle and the door was once more closed (even the horses hadn't braved the weather and were still huddled in the corner of the stable), the baby finally fell asleep, allowing the others a small window of opportunity. This opportunity was destroyed when another bang flew through the air, followed by a shrill scream.

Daniel woke up instantly. His eyes snapped open as he leapt to his feet with amazing agility. Not having the patience to lower the ladder back into position, he jumped down to the ground floor. He swore loudly when his landing was not as smooth as he had planned, in his haste to intervene with whatever injustice was taking place to, and at the hand of, his kin. All this took place before Annabel had even rubbed the sleep out of her eyes.

Patsy sat up quickly once Daniel's bulk had left their side. The rags in her hair bobbed absurdly on top of her head. She slid off the bed, dragging the ladder across the floor and down into place on the ground before making her own descent. Clouded with anxiety, she missed the bottom rung and slipped, with a thud, onto her bottom. Still half asleep, Annabel fumbled down the ladder and with Patsy, rushed across to the house.

They flew through the door just in time to see Daniel throw his father across the room, away from his mother who was lying in the exact place Hetty had laid just days previously. Daniel rounded back on his father, a fierce anger in his hazel eyes. Seizing the elder man's collar he drew back his fist and thrust it square into his mouth. Blood sprayed onto Daniel's face making him look wild. Trevor only smiled. It was a terrifying smile. Blood coated his few remaining teeth as his cracked lips stretched upwards grotesquely.

Annabel, standing shocked just inside the doorway, lost her balance as Tom barged past her, pushing her to the ground like a rag doll on his quest to assist his father. With one swift, practiced movement, he grabbed the fire poker and smashed it across the back of Daniel's knees. Annabel cried out a shrieked version of Daniel's name, in a desperate attempt to warn him, but Tom was too fast. A gasp of pain left Daniel's lips and he folded to the floor.

He looked up, seemingly determined not to show the suffering in his eyes. Annabel had been looked at with hatred and disgust before, but the look Daniel gave to his father in that moment was so strong it made her very bones turn cold.

Trevor kicked out his leather booted foot, pummeling it into Daniel's stomach. He curled into a tight ball, as his brother continued to hit him with the poker. The metal clanged as Tom frequently missed in his drunken state and hit the floor beside him. The occasional thwap of the poker hitting flesh made Annabel wince as Daniel cried out. His body turned slowly black and blue. Blood seeped from his many wounds yet his eyes never shifted from his father's face. The look inside those eyes grew colder with every second, even as the strength was leaking out of him.

All of this happened in a matter of seconds.

Amidst the horror surrounding them, Patsy had sunk down to the floor to hold her frozen mother, who seemed even more distressed at the nearness of her youngest child. The haggard woman looked on with an impassive expression as her son was beaten, without uttering a single word in protest. Unable to reach the metal jug to repeat her previous attack strategy, Annabel grabbed a bucket full of ice cold water from near the door and poured the lot over the three men. Daniel spluttered and coughed, rolling onto his other side so he could breathe, finally breaking the eye contact with his father. Almost in slow motion his attackers stopped and turned towards the young girl at the door, who had been so submissive upon her first arrival but was now beginning to harden to this wretched way of life.

"You want some of this do you?" growled Tom, raising his poker once more. His grotesquely large muscles bulged with hate as his body swayed in his drunkenness.

"Think o' the money m'boy. We can't ruin her yet."

"You ruined 'er in the forest."

Trevor laughed, a rasping sound that rattled a large quantity of phlegm in his throat. It was a sound that took Annabel back to that day, filling her with fear. Tom smiled as well at Trevor's amusement. The bond between the two men was almost sick. Tom seemed always out for his father's approval, whilst his father lived to give it to him.

"I can take you to the point o' death with this poker and then jus' leave ya in the filth wi' the idiot and the animals until you're healed. The reward'd be so big by then that your folks would 'ave no choice but to sell me your fancy house."

Tom had stepped over Daniel, careful to tread on his fingers as he went. Daniel groaned and tried to grab his brother's ankle but he just shook him off. Tom stopped so close to Annabel that their noses were almost touching. His rancid breath and unwashed body filled her nostrils so strongly, she had to fight with every ounce of will power she had not to be sick. Tom, another evil grin lighting up his features, turned around and planted a hard kick to Daniel's stomach. Patsy screeched as Tom pushed past Annabel laughing. Trevor followed his favourite son like an obedient dog.

Annabel dropped beside Daniel. The sight of his limp body filled her with a sense of panic. Her heart was beating so quickly it felt as if it were in her mouth. The sound of Patsy and her mother's shrill voices were drowned out by the blood pumping rapidly through Annabel's veins and pounding inside her head. She shook Daniel's shoulder, softly at first but with increased urgency as his body remained motionless. A small drop of blood was now trickling down from the corner of his mouth.

"Daniel!" she screamed over and over again, watching his swollen, unconscious face for any signs of life. Patsy was at their side in a matter of moments, calling his name as well. In a state of utter desperation Patsy drew back her hand, slapping Daniel over the face.

"Patsy!"

But Annabel's scorn was drowned out by another loud screech from Patsy as Daniel's eyes fluttered and a bubble of blood bloomed between his lips, signaling that he was breathing. He coughed as the air rushed back through his body.

"Daniel," Annabel whispered again. Her hands fluttered uselessly over his battered body, wanting to soothe but afraid to touch him in the risk of hurting him further.

He groaned, his eyelids pressed tightly together as if he refused to open them and return to the pain of real life. Annabel let out a breath she hadn't realised she was holding.

"You're going to be alright Daniel. I'll take care of you."

His fingers twitched and, without thinking, she covered them with her own. She squeezed them lightly and he squeezed hers back, flinching as the movement caused fresh hurt. His breathing was still slightly laboured from the agony of his wounds. The strength he had put up for his father and brother collapsed in an instant.

Daniel's mother was now talking, insulting her younger son's stupidity, but Annabel had no time for her and gently stroked Daniel's hair away from his face, exactly as Billy had done to her when she had first arrived. She watched with a stirring in her breast as his features softened at her touch.

The two girls sat there for a short while watching Daniel breathe, until Patsy got back up and went over to her mother. She had turned to face the wall, her face wrinkled up in disgust.

"Why'd I produce only idiots?" she screamed at her son, breaking the heavy silence. "Why'd ya 'av to be my child?"

With these words Daniel's last ounce of composure fell away as his entire body sagged under the weight of his mother's disappointment. Giving himself over to the emotional and physical hurt of the past week, tears started to ooze from his tightly closed eyes.

"You deserve so much more than this Daniel," Annabel whispered right next to his ear. Surprising even herself she planted a light kiss on his forehead, feeling a small spark of happiness when he shifted ever so slightly closer to her.

At her mother's scorn-filled words Patsy staggered away from her. With a final, scornful glance she turned on her heel and rushed across to the stable, returning with a frantic Billy in her wake.

"Dani," he gasped as he caught sight of his younger brother sprawled out on the floor, broken and bleeding. Annabel looked at the sibling's mother, who had turned away as if ashamed when her eldest child entered the room.

Annabel felt sick with anger.

Billy bent down without hesitation – he had come to terms with his parent's hatred before he could even walk - and scooped Daniel up with ease. He was a lot stronger than Annabel had thought. She hadn't noticed before the muscles that ran up his arms too, larger even than Tom's although Billy would never have thought to use them to inflict hurt on anyone. Daniel screamed in pain as the movement jostled his bruised flesh. When Billy had disappeared back into the stable next door, Patsy picked up the empty bucket and disappeared to fill it up. Thus, Annabel found herself alone with the woman who was supposed to care for and love her three best friends. She saw red. She was angrier than she had ever been in her life. Her blood boiled up in her veins until it reached a feverish heat.

Taking three deliberate steps towards the old woman she drew back her hand and struck it across her frail cheek so hard a prickling pain radiated up her arm. Almost instantly a red mark appeared upon her victim's face. Leaning in close to her she whispered; "this is the beginning of the end for you. I will be found soon and when I am back amongst my power and my riches I will drag you down so much further than you've taken me. That's a promise."

Snatching up a deformed loaf of bread and a few shirts from a toppling pile, Annabel turned and fled back to the stable in the wake of her friends. It was a mark of how much she had changed that she didn't run away. This was the first time she had been unsupervised, she could have done it. Yet, her heart wouldn't let her. She was too invested now. She cared too deeply.

Daniel wasn't strong enough to climb the ladder so Patsy had cobbled together a bed of loose straw, placing a tattered blanket at the top in the absence of a pillow. Daniel groaned in pain again as he was set down. Blood soaked his thin white shirt, his torso being the main area of attack, and there was a vicious lump on his head, the bruise from which had already forced his right eye shut.

Annabel wanted to cover him with her own blanket but feared it would only irritate his exposed wounds so left him for the time being to be soothed by the cool night air. As soon as Daniel was placed amongst the straw Billy picked up the baby, who cooed contentedly, wrapped in his loving warmth. Annabel didn't want to leave Daniel alone so sat beside him. She watched Billy dote on the child, refusing to allow any of them to feed her, change her or bathe her. They were only allowed the occasional cuddle and even then it was only for the short periods of time it took Billy to wash, toilet and eat. Annabel thought Billy must only be getting a couple of hours sleep a night. Even though it had been only a few days, he had begun to literally live for Genevieve. He loved her more than any father had ever loved their child.

"Billy?"

"Yeah?"

"You and Jen have to sleep upstairs on your own to-night."

"No," he shook his head. "We be lonely."

"But Tom and Trevor cannot get Genevieve if you are upstairs. Jen cannot be seen Billy."

He looked as if he would protest until Genevieve cooed again, attracting his attention. He pondered the idea Annabel had presented.

"Thinking," he muttered and Annabel kissed his cheek, earning a smile before he nodded and ascended the ladder, Genevieve in one arm, the other gripping the rungs with a practiced ease.

Annabel looked up at the sound of the door creaking open to find Patsy, laden with the now full bucket, coming back in. She put the bucket down beside Daniel. As the water's ripples diminished Annabel ripped a section of the old shirt she had stolen, dipping the fraying strips into the cold water. She unbuttoned Daniel's shirt and began to press the wet material against these wounds first. Daniel cried out the second she touched the first mark, his muscles clenching beneath her touch. Her cheeks flushed as she began to clean away the blood, revealing the tanned, scarred skin beneath it.

Patsy tried to soothe her older brother by humming. It was slightly out of tune and thus didn't hold the magic of Daniel's song. Having cleaned this part of him, Annabel washed each of his rough hands in turn, more to touch them than a need to actually be cleaned. Once she had completed this, she washed off his face. His laboured breath turned steadier as she soothed his hurt. Satisfied she had done all she could for the moment, Annabel turned to Patsy who had curled up in a ball in the corner. From a slight distance you would think she was completely at ease, drifting back into sleep as if her rude awakening had been caused by a loud bird. However, this close to her Annabel could see Patsy's eyes wide open and roaming as if she were looking for answers on the grimy wall. Annabel reached around her friend to clasp her hands in comfort; they were trembling slightly and as cold as death itself.

"Are you okay?" Annabel whispered into Patsy's ear, finding her own solace in Patsy's presence whilst trying to restore some heat into her icy fingers. She nodded, her face making a rustling sound against the straw. Patsy squeezed Annabel's hand in hers as the warmth slowly returned.

"What are you thinking?" she asked.

Annabel pondered this question for a while before answering.

"That no-one should live like this."

"No-one else does," Patsy replied.

Annabel propped herself up on her elbow, looking into the half of Patsy's face that wasn't pressed into the straw.

"Yes they do...even in my world."

Patsy turned around.

"Other people live like this? Really?" She sounded almost hopeful.

"In some sense, yes."

"But not really in your world, it's too...perfect."

Annabel laughed humourlessly.

"No it's not. It's easy, that doesn't mean it's perfect."

"Same thing," Patsy whispered turning back over and resuming her former position.

"Patsy there are violent men in every class. I've known of people who have had husbands or fathers who abused them for years but there was nothing anyone could do about it because they were too powerful. Like your father, everyone was scared of them. They play their game too well."

"It's not a game." Patsy retorted, rolling back around again to face Annabel.

"You won't be here forever Patsy. When I get taken back home, whether it be days or years from now, you're coming with me - you, Billy, Jen and Daniel if he wants to. In fact, anyone you want can come. I've got enough money and a big enough house. Lord, I have an entire wing to myself that the whole village could fit into and still have rooms spare."

Patsy's face lit up and then dimmed in disbelief.

"You don't mean it. You jus' want me to help you escape."

"Of course I mean it! How dare you say that." Annabel crawled closer to Patsy and took her hand again. Both girls were now sat bolt upright, looking each other dead in the eye.

"Really?" Patsy whispered. "I could really come with you?"

"You're like my sister Patsy...better than sister because I actually like you. You've given me the hope I needed to stay alive, I need to give it back to you somehow, some-day."

Patsy looked radiant with expectation. Her hold on Annabel was so tight it hurt but she couldn't care less. A silent tear landed on their clasped hands, glistening in the pale moonlight as if sealing their agreement. Drunk on each other's naive optimism, they both laughed. The sound hit their ears in a hollow echo. Patsy leaned back against the slimy wall and glanced over Annabel's shoul-der. Annabel followed her gaze towards Daniel. There, they watched his chest rise and fall, his fingers twitching as he dreamed, until the pale sun shone back through the broken window.

Patsy fell asleep not long after the sunrise, still leaning against the wall, her head resting on Annabel's shoulder. Annabel briefly closed her eyes but the second her lids met, blocking out the visual world, images of the fire pok-er smacking into Daniel filled her mind, flashing in front of her like a storm. She heard his first groan of surprised pain, the sound of the air leaving his lungs at the impact of Tom's boot and sleep became impossible to achieve.

Gently easing Patsy's head from its resting place, An-nabel crept over to Daniel. Sitting beside him, she ran her eyes over the scars criss crossing his torso. The recent ones were bright red and angry, whilst the old ones were pink, raised slightly above the healthy skin. Annabel jumped as he let out an anguished groan. Still in the clutches of a dream, his eyes flew open.

"No," he repeated over and over again, the exclamation getting increasingly more anguished. Annabel placed a hand on his shoulder, keeping him lying down. He took her hand in his, trying desperately to sit up.

"Daniel, wake up." Annabel tried to stir him from his dream, from his nightmare.

"No, please let me help," he continued. "I've gotta help."

"Shh, Daniel not now. You need to sleep now. Everything will be alright in the morning." A n n a b e l brushed his hair from his eyes once more and saw him relax somewhat.

"In the morning," he whispered, ceasing his fight to rise.

"Yes Daniel, it will all be better in the morning."

Chapter Thirteen

Annabel didn't sleep anymore that night. She watched Daniel, his face finally peaceful as he slept, her fingers rhythmically combing through his soft, blonde hair.

Patsy awoke first, her breathy laugh finding Annabel's ears a few hours after sunrise. She looked up.

"What?" she asked, offended that Patsy seemed to be laughing at her. She wiped her chin, afraid she had something on her face.

"Our hair looks so silly! I'd forgotten 'bout it!"

Annabel's hands went to her head. Feeling the rags still secured in her hair, she laughed as well.

"Turn around," she said, walking over to Patsy and taking down her hair. Looking at Patsy once her hair was falling past her shoulders again, she smiled. The now tight curls complemented her face shape, making her look as innocent as her youthful features should. Patsy untied Annabel's own hair, watching with her mouth slightly agape as it tumbled down into its usual dark blonde spirals, her blue eyes glittering.

"You're so beautiful," she said, wrapping one of Annabel's curls around her short finger. "Stick out like a sore thumb 'ere."

"You're not so bad yourself," Annabel replied tweaking Patsy's nose and making her way back to Daniel.

Finding him still asleep she rewashed his healing wounds. They looked less aggressive already although, his emotional scars would no doubt remain with him forever.

It wasn't until evening was once more drawing in that Daniel finally stirred.

Still half unconscious, he moaned. Annabel jumped up. Crouching by his side she placed a hand on his forehead as she had seen other people do – she didn't know what a too hot forehead felt like but she figured it would appear as if she knew what she was doing.

"You're alright Daniel, just like I promised."

He groaned again and Annabel ran her fingers slowly through his fair hair, remembering how much this had healed her when she had been hurt.

That's when she remembered. The smell of Daniel was that same soapy, musky smell that still clung to the thinner of her two blankets, the one she had been bundled inside after she had tried to escape. She realised the hazel eyes she had seen in her brief moment of consciousness weren't Billy's at all...they were Daniel's.

Daniel was her savior. He had helped her in the darkest hour of her life. He had helped her without even knowing her name. Sat there, amongst the straw and the horses, Annabel made a silent vow. She would help Daniel in whatever way she could, until the drawing of her final breath.

Leaving a few minutes Annabel filled a cup and held it up to Daniel's lips, coaxing him to drink. Whilst he was drinking Annabel realised he wouldn't have the strength to chew through the now stale bread. With a stroke of inspiration, she filled another cup of water and soaked the bread before feeding it to Daniel, like a bird nourishing its children.

Following his limited meal he quickly fell back into unconsciousness.

Carefully removing the blanket from under his head Annabel threw it over his half naked body, fearing he would become too cold during another night. Through much argument she managed to persuade Patsy to follow Billy and Genevieve up to the loft, promising she would sit with Daniel.

Annabel, having had next to no sleep in days, felt tired to her very bones. Each limb felt as if it were made of iron. Yet she had an unspoken duty to stay awake, in case Daniel needed her.

In order to think about anything else, Annabel went over to the horses. They were a little restless. Their hooves scrapped across the floor, their ears pressed back against their heads. She laid her hand on their silken shoulders, patting gently as she had done with the glistening thoroughbreds that were kept at the manor. Before long, in her sleep deprived mind set, she found herself talking to them as if they could hear her. It was then that she finally understood the appeal of animals. The fact they seemed to listen to her every utterance, without there ever being the fear they would repeat or judge her words, was intensely relieving. She was only broken out of this one sided conversation when Daniel groaned again, louder this time, showing that he had reentered consciousness in some form. Annabel rushed to his side, refilling the cup of water in case he should want it.

"No," he croaked as Annabel lifted the cup to his lips. He looked pained, almost embarrassed, as he opened his eyes. The swelling of his right eye had gone down significantly due to the hours Annabel had spent pressing a cold, wet cloth to the area. Daniel looked at the stable door with meaning in his expression. Misinterpreting this meaning Annabel rested a tender hand on his arm.

"You're safe, it's alright."

He shook his head and tried to roll onto his front in an attempt to stand but Annabel gently pushed him back down.

"You've got to rest Daniel."

"No," he clutched his side, gasping as his struggle jostled one of his wounds. "I've gotta...go."

He broke off blushing, looking at the door again. Annabel caught on, covering her mouth with her hand.

"Oh," she giggled. "Um...I'll help you..."

A trace of a smile formed on Daniel's lips at the awkward situation as he managed to raise himself into a seated position.

Annabel bent her knees and Daniel put his arm around her shoulders. She lifted him onto his feet with a grunt as his weight rested almost entirely on her right side. Daniel was shaky on his legs, his face now crumpled with both the pain and exertion. Despite the hurt, Daniel attempted a laugh when the blanket fell away, revealing his naked chest.

"Couldn't wait...to get me...naked," he rasped.

Annabel blushed. "You were hurt," she reasoned.

"That's...what they all say...ow..." He groaned as he took his first step.

"Do you want my help or not?" Annabel teased to take his mind off the hurt.

"Sorry."

With Annabel's assistance he managed to hobble outside, almost falling on several occasions. It seemed he must have damaged his ankle when he jumped from the loft; he was unable to put much weight on it at all.

Once outside of the stable Annabel waited in the doorway as he used the wall to support his way around the back. He wouldn't let her help him any further. A few minutes later he reappeared and Annabel resumed her position at his side, lowering him back onto the straw. They were both slightly out of breath and shared a cup of water between them.

"I can't drink too much," he said after a few mouthfuls.

"Why not?" Annabel asked.

"Tha' was too much effort. I don' wanna repeat it soon."

They both laughed until Daniel grimaced, clutching his side.

"I like your hair like that," he whispered after a few moments, settling back on the straw. Annabel smiled involuntarily as she felt a blush colour her cheeks. "Don' pretend to be embarrassed. I'm sure you've been told tha' by much more important people than me."

Annabel thought about that for a moment and realised whilst this was true, her vanity had always accepted those compliments as a given, of course she was beautiful. But Daniel thought she looked nice whilst she sat there at her very worst. It made her heart flutter in a strange, foreign way that, Annabel thought, was very pleasant.

"Thank you," she whispered.

They looked at each other for a while before Daniel grimaced again and squeezed his eyes shut, pulling the blanket up to his neck. He glanced at Annabel who had crossed her arms in an attempt to keep in her own warmth.

"Take the blanket Anna," Daniel whispered, holding up the cloth. "When was the last time you slept? You look tired."

"A compliment and an insult in the space of a minute, thank you Daniel. I'm alright, you are in much more need of the blanket than I."

"Seriously Anna jus' take it." As if to assert his point, Annabel shivered. "Come 'ere, we'll share."

Annabel blushed deeper than she had ever blushed before and shook her head.

"No really, I'm alright Daniel. Go to sleep."

"Oh...I didn't mean...jus' you're cold is all."

There was an awkward silence between them for a few

minutes before Daniel spoke again. "I know what they did to you. I wouldn't...I'd never do tha', I won' even touch you. I'm sorry, jus' didn't want you to be cold. Please, take the blanket. You gotta sleep."

Drawing in a deep breath, the warm feeling in her heart returning, Annabel slid beside Daniel who held the blanket up for her.

The blanket was large enough for her to remain just beside Daniel, her forehead in line with the top of his shoulder.

"Thank you." Daniel whispered a short while later, just as sleep was beginning to fog Annabel's vision.

"For what?"

"For comin' 'ere, for savin' my life, for tryin' to save Hetty." He paused. "It's better with you 'ere."

"You're delusional and concussed. I liked you better unconscious." She heard his breath leave him in a quiet laugh before the darkness of sleep descended once more.

Chapter Fourteen

The next few days passed by blissfully uneventful. In accordance with the silent vow she had made, every morning Annabel woke up beside Daniel and helped him to wash his slowly healing wounds. Unexpectedly, his nearness and soft touch were starting to heal her in return, dulling the constant shame of her psychological scars.

With Daniel out of action food was hard to come by. They daren't leave the stable for fear of seeing Tom or Trevor and instilling their wrath, leaving them no choice but to go hungry. Even the residents next door were going largely without for Daniel was unable to provide their meat. Neither Tom nor Trevor could hunt. They were both too loud and impatient.

After two days with no food Billy took a chance and snuck into the forest to fill the water bucket. On his return he found a couple of sad looking apples which, the group believed, may have been the best thing they'd ever tasted. Billy, it appeared, had been used to hunger. Patsy and Daniel brought food to him when they could but it seemed he had often been forced to scavenge in the forest.

Annabel quickly forgot her own hunger. She felt a foreign sense of achievement as she cared for Daniel – as if she had been born for this very task, as if she had sat with Daniel every day of her life but simply forgotten until that moment. The coldness she had shown to the world in her old life slowly got stripped away. Her reservations chipped at until they were erased completely. She was at ease in that stable as she had never been before.

Despite the apparent calm, there was still always that sense of something brewing. A large weight seemed to hang above the stable, which grew heavier with every passing day. Daniel would be made to work again soon. It was possible he had already rested too long. This very scene had already played out so many times in his life, he knew how it ended.

Thus, four days were all Annabel could make him stay still for. He was getting anxious to go outside, wanting to prove his strength and reintroduce meat to his diet. Therefore, with Annabel on one side and Patsy on the other, they stumbled their way towards the forest, Billy hurrying in front before anyone could spot the concealed baby in his arms. Once beneath the relative safety of the trees, Daniel dropped his arms from the two women's shoulders and leant against a trunk, breathing heavily from the exertion of staying upright.

After a few minutes he lifted his eyes in determination and stood up on his own, albeit slightly shakily. He began to walk forwards, limping on his left leg. He swayed on his fifth step and grabbed the first thing he could reach – Annabel's hand, which had shot out in some hope of catching him if he fell. Patsy ran off into the forest, an idea lighting her eyes. She came back looking pleased with herself, carrying a large stick which she handed to Daniel. He laughed, thanking her and leaned the weight of his damaged leg upon it. His opposite hand remained clasped around Annabel's.

About half way to their destination Annabel lowered him to the ground at his own request where he began forming something from the plants growing out of the forest floor. When he had finished, she noticed he had made a snare. He made several more of these along their way, hoping at least one of them would yield some dinner.

When Daniel was satisfied, they climbed down the slippery slope to the stream, which was a lot more difficult than the flat forest floor for his wounded body. He fell often, scraping the palms of his hands, yet he refused to let them help him.

When they finally made it to the bank of the river Daniel collapsed onto the grass to catch his breath. Annabel and Patsy lay down on either side of him and they smiled up at the fluffy white clouds, gliding over the canopy of trees above them.

They were all in dire need of a good wash. Luckily Patsy had thought ahead and thus pulled out two bars of the malformed soap. Daniel made Annabel and Patsy close their eyes as he removed what was left of his clothes and lowered himself into the stream. He let out a suppressed screech as the water hit his torso, where the worst of his wounds resided.

Diamonds Fall

They opened their eyes again to see Daniel scrubbing the blood and filth off of his freckled skin. It was quite a sight watching the sun shine off of Daniel's fair hair as he lathered soap over its now greasy texture. All Annabel could see of him were his shoulders and arms. She watched how his muscles worked under his skin as he cleaned his clothes and body, passing the soap over to Billy who was now in the stream next to him, having handed Genevieve to Patsy. The baby whimpered and Billy glanced at her, a concerned look in his eye. To break the tension, Daniel splashed him. Both men laughed at their childish game. Before the fight was over all four of them were soaking. Although Patsy had moved away about half way through in order to keep Genevieve dry. They all laughed so much their sides ached and tears ran down their cheeks. Annabel felt elated, lighter than she had ever felt before.

Shortly afterwards, the girls were made to close their eyes once more and they heard the sucking noises of wet clothes being drawn back over wet bodies. When Annabel opened her eyes again both boys were only in their undergarments, laying the rest of their clothes in the sun to dry. Annabel's gaze lingered on Daniel for a fraction of a second too long, taking in the shape of his legs as the soaking garments stuck to them, leaving very little to the imagination. She blushed, looking away quickly as Daniel caught her gaze. Raising an eyebrow questioningly, a small, teasing smile pulled up one corner of his mouth. He clasped his hands behind his head, wincing slightly as it stretched one of his more vicious wounds. He went to cross his ankles but seemed to think better of it.

"Like whatcha see Miss Anna?"

"No, I most certainly do not! Close your eyes!"

Daniel laughed but did as he was told without hesitation, singing a jolly sounding song as he tapped his uninjured foot on the ground to an imagined rhythm. Annabel removed her clothes with as much speed as she could and jumped into the stream, splashing the men on the shore.

As her head broke the surface she could hear Daniel's deep laugh before he resumed his song. She snatched the soap off the side and began scrubbing herself and her clothes. She didn't want to put her heavy dress back on wet so she laid it down on the ground and ducked under the water again, choosing to take a swim whilst her dress dried. She wasn't particularly good at swimming, there had never been a need for it – it was not proper for someone of her standing. She realised quite quickly that swimming was much more effort than she had previously thought. She was out of breath after only a few strokes but continued to swim until her limbs burned, relishing in the feeling of her muscles stretching out, the supple flesh tightening and toning. Pausing for a while she noticed Daniel was now sat up watching her with a smile on his face.

"Thought you were making a getaway for a minute there," he teased. "But I don't think you'd get very far swimming like that."

"What do you mean?" She had thought she was doing

really well.

Still dressed in his undergarments, he lowered himself slowly back into the stream, wincing as the cool water hit his wounds again. Annabel instinctively backed away from him, covering as much of her body as she could with her hands. Daniel did not even try to approach her but simply took off, slicing through the water quickly and effortlessly in an impressive front crawl, hardly even making a splash.

"Like that," he said, careful to remain on the opposite side of the stream to Annabel who was still blushing profusely, the water up to her chin.

"Well, I don't really have much use for swimming, it isn't proper." She tilted her chin upwards, just as she would have done at the manor. She didn't like being shown up.

"Begging your pardon Ma'am," Daniel said in a mockery of Annabel's upper class dialect, bowing his head towards her and touching an imaginary hat. He splashed her again and this time she laughed, realising how ridiculous she had sounded.

"Snob," he muttered, laughing as he resumed his swim, this time a simpler breast stroke which she tried to imitate, turning it into more of a doggy paddle.

Daniel laughed again, splashing her every time she got it wrong but still keeping a few feet away from her at all times.

After a while, both their fingers now resembling small, particularly shrivelled prunes, Annabel had somewhat mastered it and Daniel heaved himself back onto the grass, with a little help from Patsy who had climbed out a good hour before.

The sun beat down on their heads; their clothes now bone dry in the heat. Annabel once more forced everyone to turn around before climbing back into her warm dress. She lay in between Daniel and Patsy, spreading her hair out behind her so the sun could dry it.

Genevieve made a small noise, not quite a cry but still a sound of discomfort.

"Jen 'ungry. Goin' for walk," Billy stated.

"I'll come with you," Patsy said as she got to her feet, brushing the back of her skirt to rid it of any dirt.

"Mind if I stay 'ere?" Daniel asked, wincing as he shifted.

"I'd mind if you came Dani. Rest."

"Jen wanna see forest," Billy said, interrupting Daniel's laughter.

"Well Jen, check the snares for me."

"She will," Patsy giggled, swatting her brother on the head.

Once they were on their own, Annabel and Daniel lay side by side, feeling the sun gently warm their faces. The only sound was their slow breathing.

Although Annabel had been close to Daniel for days now, she quickly became very aware of his body beside her, in a way she had never felt before. His hand seemed to give off a strange heat, radiating through hers only an inch away. A light breeze rustled the leaves above them.

They watched as one fell, shining emerald green in the light as it spun through the air. It landed at the base of Annabel's neck. Propping himself up on one elbow, grimacing at the pain, Daniel leant forwards and picked it off, brushing his fingers over Annabel's skin with a deliberate slowness. His face turned serious and he bent down a little further, pressing his lips against hers.

They had barely touched yet a fire ignited itself within her.

Daniel focused his gaze on Annabel's, a frown returning to his face as he misinterpreted her motionless stature.

"Do that again," Annabel whispered.

Daniel laughed softly, their breath mixing together in the small space between them. He placed his rough palm against Annabel's cheek and touched his mouth once more to hers. This time he pressed just that little bit harder and a sound escaped his mouth. Annabel pulled away, a look of concern in her eyes. Daniel looked crestfallen.

"What's wrong?" Annabel asked, tracing her fingers over the almost healed bruise on the side of his face. "Did I hurt you?"

He laughed, shaking his head. A blush rose slowly up his neck.

"No, I - I liked it."

"Oh, I thought you were hurt."

Smiling, she kissed him once more. As he began kissing her too, he slid his fingers into her damp hair. She ran her own palms over his back, this time smiling at the small moan this brought to his lips. They were oblivious to everything around them, only breaking away from each other when their need for air became too strong to resist. They rested their foreheads together, drunk off their own happiness and laughed softly.

"Billy and Patsy should be back soon." Daniel pulled himself up into a sitting position. "They've been gone ages, so they must have found some good rabbits."

"Should – should we build a fire then?" Annabel said clearing her mind to attempt normal thought. Daniel smiled.

"You're learning! Yeah, I'll get wood."

He brushed her lips with his own one more time and then stood up, hobbling into the dense forest around them. Just before he disappeared he looked back at her and chuckled, as if in disbelief. Annabel sat on the grass in a daze with her fingers pressed against her lips, marvelling at how his had felt there. She could still taste him; still feel his hands on her skin. A thrill ran through her blood as she saw his lean frame stagger back into the clearing.

By this time, Patsy and Billy were also returning. In Patsy's arms was a large pot. Lowering it to the ground, Annabel saw it contained a knife, three dead rabbits and a few muddy potatoes.

"We wen' back for the pot and knife but we found the 'tatoes in the woods. The rabbits were in your traps Dani. Oh and we fed Jen."

Daniel lit the fire by piling dry leaves and grass on top of the wood and striking two stones together in a practiced fashion. Patsy and Billy skinned and gutted the rabbits whilst Annabel was given the task of removing the meat from the bones. The others laughed at Annabel's squeamishness during this task. They rinsed the potatoes in the stream, filling up the bucket with just enough water to cover the food and placed the pot on the heat as Daniel got back into his clothes.

The mood that evening was one of pure joy. Annabel had never thought she could feel like this with nothing more than a humble meal and the company of people she could now call her friends.

They ate so much stew they thought they would burst, drinking from the stream when the need struck them. They sang songs, told jokes and danced around the fire until they were too dizzy to stand. Anybody watching would have thought them drunk or insane but they were just young, completely oblivious to anything other than themselves and the simple happiness of this moment.

As the darkness grew heavier, their hearts turned cold with the knowledge they would have to return, for surely someone would notice their absence soon if they had not already. Climbing back up the rocks they went into the dense trees in pairs, clinging to each other and giggling with childish fears of shadows, each trying to scare the others.

Annabel and Daniel quickly dropped behind due to Daniel's injured leg. Annabel secured her arm around Daniel's waist, supporting him as he walked. He in turn wrapped an arm around her shoulders. Every time he touched her, the memories of Trevor's foul touch were replaced by this new, thrilling tenderness.

"Follow me," Daniel whispered in her ear, turning around so they were heading back towards the stream.

"Where are we going? Daniel, this is the wrong way."

"Jus' trust me."

Annabel's eyes roamed ahead of her as she scanned the forest for signs of where they could be heading. Daniel led them back down the steep bank to the stream and continued parallel to it for another few minutes.

"Here we are," he declared, stopping.

"Where's here? I don't see anything."

Daniel let go of Annabel and bent forwards, moving the branch of a tree that had begun to grow down the bank. Behind it Annabel noticed a large hole, almost like a human sized burrow. A cave of sorts.

"What is it?" Annabel asked.

"Home," he answered.

"Did you make this?" Annabel looked around as she walked inside the hide out, bent double so she could fit. It wasn't very deep, but it was large enough for them to both sit easily inside of it, a safe enough distance from the entrance.

"Nope. It was already here. I made it a little bigger though."

The den was dark, smelling of rich earth and Daniel. There was a blanket spread over the ground to form a sort of carpet and another one bundled up in the corner.

Annabel looked outside, watching the moonlight reflecting off of the stream that gently trickled through the trees.

"It's beautiful."

"Mhmm."

Annabel looked over at Daniel who was sat a few inches away from her, the whites of his eyes glistening in the shadows.

"I come here to think," he told her. "When everythin' is too much. When I can't stand it no more."

"Then...why have you bought me here?"

"'Cuz you're in my every thought anyway."

Annabel smiled as Daniel leant forwards and kissed her again. She rested her head on his shoulder.

They sat like that for about an hour, until Daniel shifted again, moving towards the entrance and holding out his hand. Annabel took it, following him to the stable.

When they arrived back, Genevieve was fast asleep in Billy's also unconscious arms down beside the horses. Patsy was nowhere to be found.

Daniel collapsed onto the floor almost as soon as they were through the doorway, his exhaustion clear in his eyes.

"Will you stay with me again Anna?" he asked.

"Always."

Chapter Fifteen

The next day, despite the healing he still had to undergo, Daniel had to resume his chores. Thus, he left at the first light of dawn, not returning until just before dusk. As soon as she saw him heading towards her at the end of the day, Annabel ran to him. All day she had been thinking about the kiss, her entire body tingling with anticipation. The feeling grew stronger with every hour Daniel wasn't in her sight. Taking his hand she led him back toward the woods. She knew what she was about to do was rushed. It went against everything she had ever been taught. Yet she needed this. She needed to take back control - not only of her life, her future, but also her body.

"Come with me. I - I want to try something. You make me better Daniel. Every time you touch me, I get better."

"Where are we going?"

"Trust me," she laughed.

"You're in a good mood."

"I'm with you. Why wouldn't I be?"

Daniel chuckled, limping along beside her.

She led them, with directions from Daniel, back towards the den.

"Can you kiss me again?" she whispered, standing directly in front of him when they reached the entrance.

Daniel placed his hands on either side of her face, drinking in her features with a look so full of love Annabel almost didn't understand it. He crushed his soft mouth over hers whilst his hands ran down her arms, spreading trails of electricity everywhere he touched. Her hands began to wander as well, tentatively at first, resting on his back then creeping beneath his shirt to feel the warmth of his skin on her palms. As the kiss deepened she pressed herself against him. Annabel stumbled backwards, turning to scramble inside the den. Clumsily she undid the buttons running down Daniel's front as he appeared inside as well, desperate to feel more of his warm skin. Her shaking fingers took an age to pull the small buttons through their fraying holes. He broke away, undoing his trousers and kicking them to the side, catching his foot as he did so and stumbling forwards. Annabel caught him, laughing as they toppled over. Daniel's warm body was soon pressed on top of her, his lips caressing her neck. Despite the tenderness of Daniel's touch, Annabel froze. Panic filled her system as she remembered the last time she had been in such a situation.

"Anna?"

Annabel's mouth had gone dry. She tried to swallow, squeezing her eyes shut. Daniel's thumbs made little circles on her cheeks, bringing her back to the present. She opened her eyes.

"I'm sorry. I just, I remembered with – with him."

Daniel looked horrified and Annabel closed her eyes again to block out his expression, regretting her reaction.

"Hey...Anna, look at me," he whispered and Annabel felt his lips touch her forehead. She opened her eyes but twisted her head to the side, still avoiding his gaze.

"I'm sorry."

"You 'ave nothin' to be sorry for. I'm not makin' you do anythin' Anna. You say the word an' I'll go outside. We don't 'ave to do this. I promise."

"I want to Daniel."

"Please Anna, don' jus' 'cuz you think I wanna."

"No listen to me Daniel." Annabel lay back again to look into his eyes once more. "I want to be as close to you as I can get. Being with you makes me happier than I have ever been in my life. It makes me forget. I need you."

Daniel smiled and placed another kiss on Annabel's forehead.

"I'd never hurt you Anna."

Annabel groped downwards and pulled the dress from over her head. The awkwardness of the gesture broke the tension in the air and dissolved them back into easy laughter. This time when his body pressed against hers she only kissed him that bit harder, her hands running once more over his bare skin.

Annabel couldn't believe she could be this happy. She had heard this was a means to an end, for married people only and nothing enjoyable. Yet she and Daniel fit together like two pieces of a puzzle, lost in their own world, each revelling in the others' pleasure. He kissed every inch of her, gazing into her eyes with so much love it caused her to cry out against his mouth, arching her back.

They lay for a long time afterwards, tangled up in each other's arms. Daniel held her close to his side, running his fingers up and down her spine. Annabel traced his scars, marvelling in the unconventional beauty of the man beside her. It was like this that they both drifted off into the best night's sleep they would ever have.

Annabel awoke sometime later, the smell of earth rich in her nostrils, countered deliciously by the warmth of Daniel at her side. Leaning up on her elbow she kissed his sleeping mouth then dressed quietly and climbed outside. She washed her face in the cool water and sat down on the bank, watching as the sun slowly rose above the trees, turning the sky shades of bright orange and pink.

As the sun finally shone down, sparkling off the clear water, Daniel appeared rubbing the sleep from his eyes. He wrapped his arms around her from behind and kissed her neck.

"Morning," Annabel whispered.

"An' what a beautiful morning it is."

They both chuckled.

"We should get back," Daniel said after a while.

"Yeah, Patsy and Billy will be wondering what happened to us."

They sat by the stream for another few minutes before they deemed it time to return. Annabel wrapped her arm back around Daniel's waist to help him climb up to the forest. His limp was ever so slightly less pronounced than the day before, his cuts a little less raw.

Daniel and Annabel parted ways just before the stable. When Annabel entered she grinned at Patsy inanely. Patsy didn't smile back.

They sat for a while listening to the birds in the trees high above their heads. The rafters creaked as Billy rolled over in his sleep and Patsy glanced sideways at Annabel.

"Why are you so quiet?" Annabel asked after a while.

"It's him."

"Who?"

"Daniel. Whatcha doin' with 'im?"

Annabel blushed profusely and shifted on the dusty floor.

"Um...well we...it wasn't planned."

"Well stop." Patsy looked at her full in the eye with obvious anger.

"What?" Annabel looked back with disbelief. "Why? He's – we're happy."

"Yeah, but you'll be jus' as happy when you leave an' marry that fiancé back in your big 'ouse and forget all about Daniel."

"Don't be absurd, I couldn't forget him – or you - even if I wanted to. I'm a different person now Patsy, I don't want to marry Theodore. I want Daniel. Please believe me. I've never felt this way before."

"An' how's that gunna work? Your rich folks gunna let you marry a poor boy? I don't think so."

"Patsy we only – who's talking marriage? I-"

"Theodore's talkin' marriage Anna. Does Dani know

you're engaged?"

"No, not yet, but it doesn't matter -"

"It'll matter to him. Tell 'im, or I will."

"Patsy – you can't."

"You're a good person Anna, an' I understand why you did it. I really do, but he's my brother, I 'av to look out for 'im."

"But that's...no, I forbid you-"

Patsy scoffed.

"You forbid me? Your upper class shit won' work 'ere! I forbid you to mess around wi' my brother Anna, you hear?"

"I'm not messing around Patsy. Why are you being so impossible? I thought you would be happy for us!"

"If you were anyone else Anna I would be, you may not think it now but when you're back with your folks you'll let him down. You've already cheated on your fiancé the first chance you got."

"That isn't how it is Patsy and you know it!" Annabel was furious now. Angry tears were building up in her eyes, her throat burning. "I love him. I'm not just messing around!"

"Maybe not on purpose Anna but you are."

Annabel sat with her mouth slightly open, staring at her friend in disbelief. So this is what it felt like to be betrayed. It felt like a rusty knife had been speared through her chest that Patsy kept twisting.

"Jus' this once Anna, don' be selfish."

Their conversation was cut short when Billy's footsteps padded across the loft. They could hear him talking to Genevieve before he appeared on the rickety ladder next to them, crouching down once he reached the floor to devour his own helping of stew. Patsy greeted him with warmth, disguising her previous coldness towards Annabel completely.

When Daniel entered the stable that afternoon he broke out in the most heartbreakingly large smile the second he laid eyes upon Annabel. He sat down beside her, wrapping his fingers gently around hers.

In Daniel's presence Annabel found herself suddenly awkward. The memories of the previous night now held a more sour tone following Patsy's words. How was she being selfish? She thought that was what love was all about...if that's what this was.

"I'm gunna come see you tonight okay?" Daniel whispered so only Annabel could hear. She nodded.

"I've gotta check on Mama now," he continued. "An' they'll have things for me to do but I'll be 'ere."

Annabel smiled but turned her head to the side when he leant in to kiss her, causing his lips to brush her soft cheek instead. Frowning slightly in confusion he got up and followed Patsy through the door, leaving Annabel once more alone, surrounded by heavy silence.

Genevieve was passed onto Annabel for the latter half of the day, following Billy being called out to deal with the horses and other farm yard animals dotted around the village.

Genevieve screamed most of the time without Billy.

However, Annabel managed for the first time to rock her to sleep just before Daniel found her that evening. He came up behind her, wrapping his arms around her waist.

"Evenin' m'lady," he whispered in her ear, kissing her neck.

Annabel couldn't help but smile at the feel of his safe arms around her as she leant back against him.

"How was the outside world?"

"Fine. Heard nothin' from Mama. She walked righ' by me, probably wouldn't even 'av been bothered if I'd been killed." Annabel flinched at Daniel's blasé manner of speech.

"She was really upset when you'd been hurt."

Daniel snorted.

"No, she was upset that I'd punched Trevor."

"Was a good punch though," Annabel reasoned.

Daniel laughed quietly. His breath tickled her skin.

"Are you okay?" he asked suddenly serious. "You seemed different wi' Patsy. Did she say summit? She's jus' scared I'll get hurt again, that's all."

"No - no, Patsy's fine. She's just protective. I'm alright, really."

"Okay, well I made you a present," he said, changing the topic. Annabel placed Genevieve in her nest like structure and faced Daniel, grinning.

"Ohh, what is it?"

Daniel reached down into his pocket, extracting a smooth piece of wood, the exact same size as his palm. The carving was very elaborate, depicting miniature faces of Billy, Patsy and Daniel. It was phenomenal craftsman-ship, the kind Annabel would never have expected to see outside of her own manor.

"It's amazing," she breathed. "Thank you."

"Really? You like it?" he sounded surprised.

Annabel gave him a rare, full smile, revealing all of her perfectly straight teeth.

"I really need to learn how to repay you...and Patsy, she made that blanket for me, oh and Billy. You've all done so much."

"You can do this," and with that he kissed her again, igniting her whole body with electricity once more.

"I can't do that to Billy and Patsy!"

They both laughed, so tightly wrapped in each other's arms they didn't notice Patsy come in until she tapped Annabel on the shoulder, making both her and Daniel jump about a foot in the air.

"What the hell Patsy!" Daniel exclaimed. "Ain't you got any sense of timin'?"

Patsy looked furious.

"Yes, I do." She gave Annabel a pointed look.

Annabel tried to shake her head so that Daniel wouldn't see, barely moving at all. Patsy glared at her.

"Has Annabel told you yet?"

Annabel's jaw dropped.

"Told me what?" Daniel looked between Patsy and An-nabel, an expression of confusion creasing his brow.

"Tell him Anna."

"I can't - Daniel it isn't what it is going to sound like - I can't imagine my life without you, I need you more than I've ever needed anyone-"

"Get to the point Anna," Daniel interrupted, the crease between his eyebrows deeper than ever.

"Before I came here - before you, I - I was engaged to be married."

Daniel looked stunned and dropped his arms immediately off of Annabel.

"I just thought you should know." Patsy whispered, looking sheepish.

Daniel was silent, his face stony in anger and disbelief.

"No, you would've said. This can't happen twice. You're not, you're not engaged." He caught the panicked look on Annabel's face and backed away. "No. So - so this was all a joke for you?"

Annabel's eyes misted over in tears.

"No, I just – I forgot."

It was a disgustingly feeble excuse. She was ashamed of herself as soon as it had passed her lips.

"You forgot?! Is that what you'll do about me – just forget?" His voice sounded thick, his eyes focused just above her head as if he were unable to meet hers. "I'll jus' be that stupid poor boy that fell in love with you."

"No, Daniel – please wait," she cried, but he rushed out the door, slamming it shut behind him with a bang that hung in the air with a heavy sense of finality.

Annabel suppressed a sob as she climbed the ladder to her loft. Lifting it up before she could be followed, she curled into a ball and wept.

The next day even Genevieve seemed to pick up on the atmosphere, she was inconsolable from dawn until dusk, her cries growing ever more frantic. Billy looked upset.

"Dani mad," he stated as he rocked the baby, a look of concern creasing up his face. Annabel nodded. "Billy fault?"

"No," she whispered taking his hand. "It's me, he's mad at me."

"Why?"

Annabel racked her brain for an answer to this question. "I lied to him," was the best she could come up with.

"He forgive, you see."

Annabel kissed him on the cheek.

"Thank you Billy."

He smiled at this acknowledgment and moved Genevieve to rest on his shoulder, winding her in another futile attempt to soothe her. All of a sudden she emptied her tiny stomach down Billy's back. Annabel leapt up and washed it off as fast as she could. Jen began to wail even louder.

She could tell Billy was worried about her but Annabel felt sure it was just some small ailment. She'd heard babies were sick all the time.

The following day Genevieve was even more restless.

Billy and Annabel had had next to no sleep, desperate to soothe her so that her cries would not be heard.

Her temperature had increased at an alarming rate.

Billy was frantic. He bathed her repeatedly to bring down her fever, feeding her as much as she would take which, in her current state, wasn't a lot. Her little limbs kicked out, thrashing against the illness she had no understanding of.

She needed medicine but Annabel had no idea how to acquire it. She searched desperately for Daniel or Patsy but they didn't seem to be anywhere. She even asked the villagers where they were but they refused to answer. Frustrated she let out a scream towards the sky, pulling at her hair like she was deranged. A few eyes looked her way but quickly bent back to their work when she looked towards them.

Just as the darkness was once more beginning to descend over the horizon Annabel remembered the den. She took off at a run. Holding her skirt above her knees, regardless of who was watching, she darted through the trees. Her legs burnt, her lungs drawing in deep, rasping breaths as she pushed herself beyond her physical limit. Finally reaching the bank, after taking several wrong turns, she slowed to a walk in order to gain her bearings. She noticed him almost immediately. Daniel looked up, alarm crossing his features. He clambered to his feet, his ankle still visibly weak.

"What do you want?" he spat, his voice full of fury.

"I need help." Her voice sounded foreign as it fought to gain purchase over her lungs, sucking desperately at the air around her.

"I can't give it. Find Patsy."

"I can't, I can't find her. Please."

He tried to walk away but his ankle gave out, forcing him back against the bank.

"Goddamn it Anna, why me? Why did ya 'ave to mess wi' me?"

Annabel hated the defeated look in his eyes as he ran a hand through his dishevelled hair.

"Is my life not bad enough?" he concluded.

"Daniel I-" She wiped a tear from her cheek in frustration. "I didn't want to mess you around, I've never even met this man I'm meant to marry. I – us – it felt good."

He laughed without humour. "Yeah, sure."

"Stop being so defeatist Daniel! You're the most amazing person I have ever met and I am a selfish, vain, pretentious mess! I'm horrible and I know it, you and I both know you can do better than me." Daniel laughed again, looking back up at her.

"This isn't about us Daniel, please. I promise I will explain it all later. Can you help me for Genevieve's sake, she's sick and I don't know what to do. I'm useless in every situation here. I hate it – I won't have her die because of my own incompetence – please."

She was practically begging now, but she saw his eyes when she mentioned Genevieve and knew he would help.

"What can I do?" he asked, once more trying to stand, this time succeeding, albeit slightly shakily.

"She needs medicine, I don't know what type but she isn't well. Is there anything here that can help her? Just tell me where it is and I'll go get it myself. You're still too weak, it will be quicker if I go."

Daniel considered this, running a worried hand back through his hair. "There's a wooden box under Mama's bed. He dunno 'bout it. What's Jen got?"

"I – I don't know, she's really hot and she's breathing really strangely. Um, she's been sick a few times, can't keep any food down longer than an hour."

"Patsy had summit like that. She was older, I dunno what it'll do to Jen. We used a green bottle, don' even know if it's still good but it's worth a shot."

"Thank you," Annabel muttered.

Seeing Daniel so worried the ache to touch him grew too much. She closed the distance between them and kissed him quickly on the cheek. Before she could see the expression on his face she ran back towards the house.

In her haste, Annabel had forgotten to come up with a plan. There was no time to be worried so she hesitated for only a few seconds before taking a deep breath and entering the house. Her naive mind, so accustomed to simply taking what she wanted, thought she could simply walk in, find the medicine and return it the next day without being seen.

The first step happened smoothly. She managed to get into the house without detection, making her way into the second room, which turned out to be a cramped, stuffy bedroom. There was only one bed, the mattress made of straw and the frame made badly from roughly chopped wood. It looked as if it had been broken several times.

The floor was covered in small, moth eaten blankets.

Wrinkling her nose against the pungent scent of stale sweat and alcohol, a slightly diluted version of Trevor's body odour, Annabel stepped over the blankets as carefully as she could. Reaching the bed she knelt down, assuming this was where Daniel's parents slept. There was a strong odour of urine coming from the stained sheets, making Annabel gag. She pushed the neck of her dress over her nose but her face was now slick with her own sweat so it wouldn't stay up.

Holding her breath and slithering beneath the bed, Annabel located the wooden box in the very back corner behind several more bundled up blankets, clothes and empty bottles. Her fingers shook slightly as she rifled through the trinkets, pulling out the green bottle with ease. She allowed herself a small smile at her achievement, experiencing a true pang of pride. She had achieved something likely to benefit another, completely on her own.

Annabel had just emerged from under the bed when she felt a hand seize her shoulder and twist her around. Pain shot through her shoulder blade as she was shoved to the floor.

She screamed as a calloused hand covered her mouth... just like the first time. She heaved at the smell of him so close to her.

"The rich girl stealing from my bedroom," he hissed. She could feel his excitement at the idea of the upper class girl driven into this ultimate form of submission.

Trevor used his free hand to start pulling up Annabel's dress. At the feel of his hand on her legs a flash of anger burst through her, such as she had never felt before.

With this sudden explosion of emotion Annabel kicked out with as much strength as she possessed, which was considerably more than when she had first arrived a few weeks ago. She connected with the place she knew would hurt him the most and he let out a high pitched yell of pain. Smirking in a way that twisted her face into an almost grotesque ugliness, Annabel clambered to her feet and seized up a rusting bucket being used as a chamber pot. It was almost too heavy to carry but her anger spurred her onwards. The contents sloshed onto the floor as she threw her arm back. When she brought it forwards there was the clang of metal colliding with bone and a spray of blood leapt out of Trevor's split skull, splattering Annabel's milky white face scarlet. She kept hitting him in a mad frenzy until another strong hand grabbed her wrist. She whirled around, about to inflict the same injury on her new attacker when she came across a pair of vivid hazel eyes. Her fingers slackened and the pot thudded to the ground, the sound muffled by the straw.

"Daniel," she whispered still caught up in a trance. Her breathing was coming out heavy, her blood pounding behind her temples. Annabel's legs gave out beneath her and Daniel, as if the move had been choreographed, caught her in his arms just before she could hit the ground.

He still didn't possess the strength to actually lift her so Daniel lowered her feet carefully onto the floor where they helped each other to walk out the door. Glancing back over Daniel's shoulder as they both stumbled outside Annabel could see Trevor's ghostly white face, contrasted dramatically by an alarming amount of deep scarlet blood. Its shine was almost beautifully in the dim, smokey light.

When they reached the stable Daniel helped Annabel onto the straw, in the exact same place he had laid her before. The memory stirred Annabel back into life.

"How – how's Jen?" she asked.

Nobody answered. Billy was hunched over the tiny baby whose cries had now stopped, her breathing heavy and laboured.

"I – I got the medicine," Annabel stuttered removing the small green bottle from her sleeve where she had managed to conceal it.

Billy grinned, placing Genevieve down as Daniel approached him. His limp was still bad. His entire body lurched as if he would fall with every step, his face a constant grimace of pain.

Annabel gave him a weak smile of thanks but he kept his eyes locked on the baby.

"How do I give it to her?" Annabel asked, holding the medicine out to Daniel who took the bottle from her hands, still avoiding her gaze.

He put a few drops of the ointment on his finger and fed it into Genevieve's mouth. He did this three times and then put the cork back in the bottle, burying it in the straw beneath them.

"An' now we wait," he said, sitting back and stretching his legs out in front of him. His ankle clicked as he moved it.

Annabel noticed he had sat as far away from her as he could.

"Daniel," she crawled closer to him, her limbs still weak from shock. "Please can we talk?"

He looked at her properly for the first time in days, his eyes widened as he took in her blood splattered face. A single drop slid down her cheek like a crimson tear.

"I...let me explain everything from the beginning Daniel, please."

His features, whilst worried, were still set in anger. His eyes fixated themselves on the ceiling as he slowly nodded.

Ignoring the fact that Billy was sat beside them, Annabel told Daniel about her entire life, from her upbringing to her betrothal and everything in between.

"I was supposed to meet him the day I got taken here. There was to be a big ball where it was going to be announced. The engagement isn't even official. For all I know he's already married to someone else by now."

Hedging her bets, Annabel inched ever so slightly closer and placed her fingers around Daniel's.

"I love you," she whispered, putting as much force and meaning behind those words as she could. "I've never said that to anyone before but I say it with all my heart. When I'm with you I feel safe, happier than I've ever felt before. You don't change me, or want me to be someone that I'm not, you simply make me better. I can't even explain it, I'm putting this terribly. I don't know what the future holds. I don't know how we will be together. All I know is we will be. I love you, so much I can barely stand it."

Without shifting his gaze from the cobwebbed ceiling Daniel's fingers tightened, giving Annabel's hand a small squeeze. Unannounced, a single sob escaped her lips in relief.

That night Daniel and Annabel stayed awake, watching Genevieve sleep. Billy fell asleep within minutes, exhausted after his sleepless night. After about an hour of listening to Billy's low snores, Daniel finally looked at Annabel, the sparkle of his hazel eyes just visible in the gloom.

"You okay?" he asked. Annabel nodded.

Very slowly he withdrew his hand from inside Annabel's and cupped it around her cheek. She closed her eyes, absorbing only the feel of him.

"Are you mad at Patsy?" he whispered.

Annabel shook her head. She had realised almost immediately it wasn't the young girl's fault. She was looking out for her brother, who had been hurt by love before. The fault was not Patsy's but Annabel's, she had been the betrayer. She couldn't stay mad at Patsy anyway, in fact, she probably loved her even more for her loyalty to her siblings.

"Everything will be alright in the morning," he muttered, repeating the very words she had told him only days previously, in this very spot.

Subconsciously Annabel shuffled closer to Daniel. Resting her head upon his shoulder she closed her eyes and listened to the regulating breath of Genevieve beside her. None of them spared so much as a thought to Trevor, lying dead only a few feet away.

Chapter Sixteen

It was just as she had given into her body's need for sleep when the noise began.

At first Annabel thought she must surely be dreaming. There was an almighty scream of anguish followed by a single pair of running feet that quickly turned into a stampede. The floor rumbled as the sounds of fear melted effortlessly into laughter. There were screeches of merriment and disbelief.

Slowly Annabel raised herself to her feet as the noise continued to increase. She poked her head out the door as Patsy, who had come in at some point during the evening, crept up to her side.

"Wha's goin' on?" she asked, rubbing the sleep out of her eyes.

"I don't know. It sounds like a festival...I mean, not that I've ever been to one, they're not-"

"Festival? Wha's tha?"

"Oh um...a celebration."

Patsy continued to look a little confused so the two women snuck outside, closing the door behind them so Billy and Daniel wouldn't wake. Emerging beside the house, keeping to the shadows so they wouldn't be seen, they caught sight of what looked like all the inhabitants of the village gathered in the square. There was a bonfire blazing in the centre with people dancing around it, holding bottles of liquor that sloshed over the sides to make marks on the muddy ground. The strangest thing of all was that every single person wore a smile. They giddily clapped each other on the back like old friends, forgetting everything in their joy. Annabel and Patsy simply looked on perplexed, until a silhouetted figure stumbled out of the house directly beside the stable. The figure was much more intoxicated than the other people, his broad build barely able to hold itself up. Annabel's heart jumped into her mouth as the man turned towards her. His face flickered with the bright orange light from the fire, tears shining on his deranged features...it was Tom.

His eyes jumped between the two females staring at him from the shadows and his nostrils flared, mucus running into his stupefied mouth.

Before he spoke a word Annabel knew he had found Trevor.

Tom stood motionless for a while, staring at them, the firelight casting shadows around him. The absence of his father at his side made him look as if he were missing a vital part of himself, like looking at a man with no limbs. He stumbled forwards and Annabel caught the smell of alcohol on his breath so strongly she gagged.

"You," he slurred, pointing somewhere slightly to the left of Annabel. "You did this!"

She shook her head.

"What - what was me? What's happened?"

She tried to feign some kind of concern, making her voice sound fake to her own ears.

"YOU KNOW WHAT HAPPENED!"

Spit flew from Tom's mouth and landed on Annabel's skin. She fought as hard as she could to keep the revulsion off her face.

"N – no I don't." She straightened up, reaching for his raw, calloused hand. "T – tell me what happened."

"YOU KNOW YA BITCH, GE'OFF ME!"

He shook her off so violently she was forced back, dropping his hand as quickly as she could. Patsy looked on at the exchange with wide eyed wonder, clenching her fists and frowning. Her eyes kept darting towards the door of the stable, dreading the awakening of her brothers.

"Please Tom, let me h-help you," Annabel stammered, her mouth was so dry her tongue stuck to the roof.

"'E's dead!" Tom screamed.

"H-how?" she asked, although she already knew the answer to that.

"You did summit, you must'a."

"With what Tom?"

Tom was getting really angry now.

"I'll tell your people. Tell 'em you're a mad woman! You'll be ruined," he hissed.

Somehow this was more menacing than if he had shouted, however the absurdity of his words made Annabel laugh out loud. The reaction surprised even herself.

"You think people would believe you over me? I'm from one of the most powerful families in the entire world and you – you're nothing, less than nothing."

She employed her best scornful tone, one she was well rehearsed at using. The effect had obviously been good as he staggered back a step as if she had slapped him.

"I'll show ya who's nothing!"

As quick as a flash his hand came up and he grabbed a fist full of Annabel's hair. A high pitched shriek left her mouth. Patsy jumped forward, hitting every part of her brother as Annabel was dragged down onto the ground. Despite the young girl's efforts, her brother was too intoxicated on alcohol and grief to feel physical pain.

Still holding onto Annabel's hair, Tom dragged her into the small, smokey house bathed almost completely in darkness. He threw her down at the foot of the bed, beneath which she had stolen the medicine just hours earlier. There were still blood stains, partly dried and congealed into large clots, on the sheets and floor.

Tom bent down, grabbing her chin, and tilted it up roughly so she was forced to look upon Trevor's face. His skin was pale, his eyes unfocused and lifeless.

"Look whacha did! Look at 'im!"

Tears were now racing themselves into his rough beard as he stumbled, falling against the wall. He looked up at her through hazy eyes, trembling with an anger so great it looked as if he would explode with it. Eventually the alcohol took its full hold over him and he slid down to the floor, crying disgustingly into his hands with great, gulping sobs.

Before he could come to his senses, Annabel got to her feet and fled the room.

When she reached the kitchen Tom's mother was bent over the fire, stirring at the pot so violently the thin stew leapt out, sizzling as the drops landed on the burning embers. Looking up she directed a look of undiluted hatred in Annabel's direction.

"Witch!" she spat. "You've ruined my 'usband an' my son!"

Annabel shook her head. "No...me and Daniel..."

"You stupid? I don' care 'bout 'im, ya ruined Tom. He were the only true child o' mine."

Annabel's mouth fell open with a small pop.

"Are you...joking? Can you not see the terror that Trevor and Tom place on everyone else in this God forsaken village? You need to wake up woman and realise their suffering is far from overdue."

The old woman stood up, so quickly Annabel would have missed it if she'd blinked, and struck her hand hard across Annabel's cheek. She stumbled back, stunned.

"Your other children are beautiful, why do you refuse to see that?" Annabel retorted when she regained the ability to speak.

"Wha', girls an' idiots? I shoulda drowned 'em soon as they were born."

"Your ignorance will leave you in the shadows whilst the rest of them bloom into the fantastic people they are. I'll see to that if it's the last thing I ever do." Annabel turned towards the door in disgust to see Daniel standing just inside the threshold, staring at his mother with a dumb founded expression on his face.

"Drowned? I've only ever tried to 'elp you. I stayed in this hell for you," he murmured stepping closer to his mother, brushing his fingers against Annabel's hand as he walked past. "I've 'unted your food since I could walk, taken your beatings wi'out battin' an eye cuz you're my mother and I wanted to help you."

"Daniel," she soothed, reaching up her hand to rest on his arm, her expression still distant and uncaring. "We can't live wi'out food. Ya gunna let your family starve?"

He scoffed. "You don' care if ya never see me again, you jus' want me to keep gettin' your food? Screw you. Listen Mama...the whole village is celebrating his accident."

"Accident! She did this!"

"How? Look at 'er, how could she have hit someone hard enough to do that much damage?" Daniel left a dramatic pause, as if he had rehearsed the whole thing in his head. "It was me."

Daniel grabbed Annabel's hand and without so much as a breath, walked back to the stable. Once inside he immediately burst out laughing. Annabel looked on a little worried.

"You were amazing!" he exclaimed, placing a hand on either side of Annabel's face and kissing her hard on the mouth.

"Daniel, wait." Annabel said, trying to make him think

straight. "You – you took the blame for me, why would you do that? Tom will kill you."

"Cuz I love you Anna, cuz I bloody love you." He laughed again, picking her up and spinning her around with a look of ecstasy on his face.

"We'll run away," he said as he put her back down. "Now."

Daniel had a serious look on his face as he gazed deeply into Annabel's eyes, searching for something.

"It's too risky."

"So's stayin'! The village's so busy, we could go without bein' noticed. We gotta go now Anna!"

"H-how?"

"We'll take the horses. Billy an' Patsy on one, you an' me on the other."

"That'd be really inconspicuous, wouldn't it?"

"I don' even know wha' tha' means." Daniel bent his head to kiss her again, "but it'll work. I feel lucky."

"We still need...we can't just...a plan of some sort. I don't know what to do, I've never-"

"How'd ya get 'ere? Wha' can ya remember?" Daniel asked, his serious expression back in place.

"Um...I'm not sure, I was unconscious and they blind-folded me. Um, we - we followed the stream I think but like I said, I only remember bits of it. I'm sorry."

"Nah, tha' good. We follow the stream."

The idea of having a plan, even with all the risks, sent a thrill of anticipation through Annabel's body. "I'm going home. Am I really going home?"

"No Anna, we're goin' home."

Daniel released Annabel now and began to pace across the floor. The straw crunched beneath his feet.

Annabel rushed up the ladder. Bending down to reach her hand in the small space between the bed and the wall, she pulled out the ornate hair comb and the carving Daniel had made for her. She wrapped them in a strip of her unworn nightgown and secured them inside the bodice of her dress.

Once she had done this she folded up the patchwork blanket made for her by Patsy, bringing it down to the ground floor, knowing they would need it to keep warm during the cold nights they would have to spend in the forest.

"Yes, tha's a good idea." Daniel mused looking at the blanket in her hands. "We won' be able to light fires, not for longer than it takes to cook, the smoke'd make us easier to find if anyone's followin' and they will be when they know we're gone. You're worth a lot o' money."

Annabel nodded. She hadn't given that a thought. It was at that moment that Patsy came back through the door looking flustered. She had disappeared when Tom had dragged Annabel into the house but no one knew where she had gone.

"Mama jus' saw me." She looked panicked. "She said Daniel killed Papa and that Tom'd kill 'im when he woke up."

"Patsy we're leaving," Daniel said, taking her hand. "Tonight...now. Anna says we gotta follow the stream, we'll take the horses and jus' go while the village is so busy, we can sneak away wi'out bein' seen. We gotta try, we got nothin' left in this place."

Patsy grinned, then frowned.

"Wha' about the boys?"

"What boys?" Annabel asked.

"Hetty's boys. I can' leave 'em."

Patsy's face was stern, only her eyes gave away her desperation to run. Annabel thought on her feet, going with the first idea she had.

"When we get back, it will only be a few days, I will tell my people where the village is. I will have the boys rescued. They can live with me too or I can pay for them to be looked after somewhere else…whatever you want to do. My family is powerful Patsy but we cannot help them from here. I know it's hard but we have to leave them, just for a few days. Tom won't hurt his sons, they mean everything to him."

Patsy opened her mouth as if to protest but closed it again and nodded, bending to fold up Billy's blanket as well.

"If someone sees us, we'll all ge' killed." Patsy whispered.

"We'll be killed if we stay. I can feel it Patsy, the violence that's shadowed our lives has peaked, it's now or never." Daniel placed a hand on his sister's shoulder. Patsy nodded again and set the neatly folded blanket down beside Annabel's, seeing the truth in Daniel's anxious words.

"We'll need food," she said. "And Billy."

"I'll get 'im." Daniel said, swiftly climbing the ladder as Patsy began to heave a cracked, creaking saddle onto the closest of the horses.

Annabel could hear Daniel treading across the rafters overhead before Billy's gentle voice started up. Billy emerged just as the horses had finished being tacked.

"Wha' Billy need to know?" he asked, confused.

"We're leavin' Billy. We're going to take the 'orses and Jen to the big 'ouse, Anna's house. We'll be far away from Trevor and Tom, we can make money an' – an' eat meat for dinner every night! Jen'll be safe to do everythin' she wants to do." Patsy explained.

Billy's eyes lit up and his face split into the most beautiful smile. "Horses come?"

Daniel nodded, squeezing his elder brother's hand. "We leave now bu' listen, we mus' be very very quiet okay? It's dangerous we're leavin', no-one mus' know. A secret."

"Yeah secret, shh." Billy put his finger to his lips and all of them grinned, giddy at the idea of their imminent rebellion.

Patsy snuck out for a last ditch attempt to gather what supplies they could, coming back with a stale loaf of bread and a water bottle made from what looked like a cows stomach. Daniel looked up, disbelief in his eyes.

"Where did you get that?" he asked, incredulous.

"Stole it. It were on a horse by the blacksmiths." Patsy shifted her feet guiltily whilst Daniel continued to look from her to the bottle and back as if she held an entire fortune in her hands, instead of the mangy looking container. He filled it with milk for the baby then strapped the blankets and supplies onto the saddles. A pair of trousers were thrown in Annabel's direction.

"Why are you giving me these?" she asked, looking at Daniel.

"You can't ride proper in a dress." He laughed at her expression and so, to avoid argument, Annabel slipped the trousers under her dress. Daniel passed her a knife and she reluctantly made a large slit up the front of her dress so she would have the room to ride properly.

"You okay?" Daniel asked once she was finished, standing awkwardly in the middle of the floor.

"Yes, just a little scared I guess."

Daniel's arms tightened as he held her for a few seconds. The warmth of his breath caressed her hair. "So am I."

Patsy went outside first, checking the villagers were all still in the square. The report was all clear so, with Daniel and Billy each leading a horse, they set off.

They couldn't have looked more suspicious if they tried; looking around them every step they took. Billy, giddy on Genevieve's miraculous recovery, had her in a makeshift sling across his chest. They were all thanking their lucky stars that she was finally fast asleep.

Daniel led Buck with one hand. His pale mane matched Daniel's own hair colour incredibly well. His other hand was tightly clasped in Annabel's.

Patsy was walking quickly out in front, her eyes darting into every crevice, jumping when the wind caused the shadows to sway.

Once inside the trees they each let out a massive sigh of relief. Billy and Daniel secured one foot in the stirrup nearest them without missing a beat and swung their legs over the huge horses with ease.

Patsy held onto the back of Troy's saddle and, with Billy's help, was hoisted up after him. Annabel took her lead and scrambled up behind Daniel, who sniggered when she was a little less graceful than she would have liked. She nudged him playfully and he laughed, breaking the thick tension of their situation. Of course Annabel knew how to ride, there were many horses back at the manor, but she had always used a mounting block and ridden side saddle. This new way of riding however, felt a lot more secure.

"Hold onto me as tight as you can and don't let go." Daniel told her. She wrapped her arms immediately around his waist, knowing they needed to get away as quickly as they could and rested her cheek against his shoulder. She saw Daniel's cheeks move and knew he was smiling. Off to their right Billy kicked his horse into action. Just before they rode out of sight, Daniel looked back, taking one final look at the only life he had ever known.

Chapter Seventeen

They galloped through the forest as if they were flying, weaving in and out of trees with perfect efficiency. Annabel could feel the muscles working beneath Daniel's jacket as he steered the horse, urging it on with gentle squeezes of his thighs.

After a few hours however the horses had become slow, froth foaming at their mouths and sweat sliding off their hair.

Billy stopped Troy, making Patsy jump down before following her to the floor. He led the horse to the stream and undid the saddle. Daniel drew Buck up beside him. His head bent down sharply towards the water making Daniel lurch forwards onto the horse's neck.

"Troy tired," Billy stated.

"Everyone's tired, we can't stop."

"Troy tired," he repeated anxiously. "Buck too."

Daniel seemed to know this was a lost battle so jumped down, lifting Annabel after him and undid the saddle as well.

"I guess it's as good a time as any to eat." He sighed, breaking off tiny bits of the bread and handing them around.

The horses grazed for a while in the darkness before they once again secured the saddles and set on their way, slightly slower this time.

"See, that's how you ride," Daniel said proudly, glancing back after they had ridden in silence for about an hour. "Lookin' good."

Annabel smiled, resting her cheek back against his shoulder as the gentle movement of the horse made her eyelids droop. They were both exhausted, having stayed up most of the night. Annabel felt herself slipping off into sleep several times, only to be jerked awake again when Troy lost his footing on concealed burrows or tree roots and stumbled.

By noon the next day they found themselves in a very dense part of the forest which they deemed a safe enough distance away from the village to afford them some rest. Annabel removed Troy's saddle and bridle, whilst Daniel limped off into the thick trees to set snares.

They would have to wait a number of hours before they could check them again so they decided to sleep, curled up together beneath the blankets. Too used to sleeping rough and far too exhausted for it to matter anyway, they were all out cold in seconds.

Daniel shook them awake just as twilight was settling back in. Warmth radiated from a freshly lit fire off to Annabel's left and the smell of cooking rabbits filled her nostrils, making her mouth water. The juxtaposition between this scene and the similar one on her first day with this family was remarkable.

Once the rabbits were cooked they tore the meat off the bones greedily. It burnt their hands and tongues but they were too hungry to care. Once the bones had been licked clean and they had filled themselves with as much water as they could, they climbed back onto the horses and rode further into the trees.

The density of the greenery increased until they were forced to slow the horses to an idle walk. As the darkness drew on, the bank of the stream became too narrow and slippery to continue along. It was with one last drink and a heavy heart that they moved away from it, vowing to find it again when the sun had risen.

There was a sense of mourning among them as the stream got further behind them. Genevieve started to whimper and then scream whilst, in stark contrast, the others walked in silence but for the breaking of small twigs beneath their feet.

They had set out so full of excitement they hadn't really thought about what a few days in the forest would be like. They were finding out all too quickly how brutal it could be.

Their muscles ached. Their bodies were fatigued from the exercise whilst their skin was clogged from their own and the horses sweat. Dirt caked their legs from the muddy ground.

Their progress was slow but Billy insisted the horses have a few hours rest. The humour that had laced the air on that first day had disappeared completely, in place of sharp tongues and tense silence, broken only by the hungry cries of the tiny baby in Billy's anxious arms. Patsy led Troy now, pulling on his reins impatiently when he tried to bend towards the lush grass at his feet. This slight mistreatment of his oldest friend had Billy stomping after his sister, shouting insults at her and thus making her even more irritated. Annabel found it best not to say anything. She knew better than anyone the hurt she could inflict with words when she was angry.

Annabel and Daniel kept their hands loosely linked together, desperate to prove their commitment to each other. In the thick silence Annabel couldn't help thinking about her life back at the manor and with it, the fiancé she would have to deal with...if he hadn't already been betrothed to someone else.

She hoped he had.

She couldn't even begin to imagine what would happen when she told her parents she wanted to stay with Daniel. They wouldn't see him as the beautiful boy who had taught her everything she knew about life and love, they would just see the poor boy who was taking away their best business asset. Her grip on Daniel's hand strengthened and he gave her a tight smile.

"What's wrong?" he whispered, as if afraid to disturb the heavy silence too much.

"Nothing. I'm just, I'm a little worried."

"About what?" Daniel's brow creased in confusion. "You're goin' home."

"I know, and I'm pleased about that, but then, part of

me doesn't want to. It's just...I can't explain it properly, not even to myself. I'm afraid of returning to the person I was, the person that is supposed to appear perfect. Yet, I'm not perfect, not even close...not now anyway."

Daniel let go of her hand, instead wrapping his arm around her shoulder and bringing her closer, so he could place his lips to the top of her head.

"You're perfect to me an' I think it'll be fine, you'll fit back in tha' world quicker than a blink."

"But, what if I don't? Seriously what if they don't like either of us? I couldn't stand it if people didn't like you. You mean so much to me."

"Exactly, I mean so much to you. No one else matters to me Anna. So long as you still love me, nothing else matters."

"I wish we could just build a house here. Grow our own vegetables, eat rabbits every day and live as one big happy family. Just you, me, Billy, Patsy and Jen."

"Annabel, your home has nothing to do with its place, it's the people you fill it with. You're heading t'ward your family - a proper family. They'll love you jus' as much as they did when you left."

Annabel smiled, leaning her head on his shoulder as they walked.

"I love you," she whispered.

"I love you too. We will be together Anna. I promise you."

At that moment, shattering the peaceful atmosphere, Patsy stopped Troy. Billy, taken by surprise, almost collided with her back. She tightened the girth of Troy's saddle and jumped on. Billy screamed.

"No, Troy resting!"

"No Billy, Patsy resting! Troy's been resting for hours. If we can't ride 'em, why are they here?"

Billy began to sulk, deliberately refusing to get up onto the horse as Daniel and Annabel mounted Buck. Annabel got bored of listening to Billy and Patsy's fighting. Pressing her ear as tightly as she could into Daniel's back she closed her eyes and tried to drown it out. Daniel, as if sensing her mood, started to hum softly. She could feel the sound vibrating through him. She pressed a kiss onto the bare skin of his neck and listened to his soothing song. The music calmed both Patsy and Billy down and soon they were all singing along to a song Annabel had never heard before...although, like all the songs Daniel sung, it fit perfectly into their surroundings.

Caving into his own exhaustion Billy clambered onto Troy, apologising to him and stroking the hair of his back, with the stubby fingers that were almost identical to his younger sisters and the complete opposite to Daniel's.

Annabel rested her palms over Daniel's heart so she could feel its steady beat. He gathered the reins into one hand, steering the horse with practiced ease, then lifted her hand to his mouth, brushing his lips over her pale skin. The earlier tense silence was lifted completely as pure contentment filled Annabel. She thought, if she could stay in any moment, this would be the one she would choose. Right there, on that horse with Daniel, she was the happiest she had ever been.

The light of a new day was now upon them, the sun shining through the thin leaves, reminding Annabel of her and Daniel's first kiss. Troy had taken Billy, Patsy and Genevieve a little further ahead into the woods so Annabel could no longer see them. She could still just about hear the heavy falls of hooves somewhere up ahead so knew they couldn't be too far away. They had also trodden a path in the leaves so there was no chance of losing them. Things were far from perfect but Annabel and Daniel were each lost in their own private universe. Daniel turned his face, briefly brushing his lips over hers. Annabel's hand slid into his hair to hold him there for a second longer. He broke away, laughing under his breath as she leant against him again and he turned to look forwards, checking they were still heading in the desired direction. Blissfully unaware of her surroundings, apart from the tender touch of Daniel's hand touching hers and his low, powerful song filling her ears, she didn't hear the extra hooves falling just out of sight in the darkness until the shot reverberated through the forest.

Buck reared in fright. Annabel and Daniel, taken unawares, were flung to the ground whilst Buck ran into the growth, carrying with him everything they needed to make it home. Both the riders were winded, gasping on the ground for several seconds. Annabel lifted herself half up into a sitting position to look at Daniel, whose face was contorted in pain.

"Daniel, what happened?"

"I dunno," he coughed, wincing.

"We've got to move. Could it be Tom? It sounded like a gun."

Sitting up, he ran a finger down Annabel's face, searching her to make sure she was okay. A small amount of blood smeared on her cheek where he touched. Annabel grasped his hand and looked at the blood on his fingers.

"You've been shot," she exclaimed, stating the obvious.

"I'll be fine, looks worse than it is." He tried to stand up but his ankle gave out beneath him and with a howl of pain he collapsed on the floor once more, clutching his arm where a red stain was growing outwards over the white fabric of his shirt.

Annabel searched the trees with her gaze, whilst simultaneously flinging her arm around Daniel's waist. She tried to help him stand but she was weak and bruised as well. They both stumbled back to the floor.

There was no sign of Troy anywhere. Annabel closed her eyes for a split second, hoping he had taken his charges far away from here. Startled, Annabel heard a voice through the growth and clutched onto Daniel's waist tighter.

"FREEZE!"

She looked down at Daniel, wondering how soon they could hide. Although, even as she thought this she knew it would be futile; they were unarmed and had already been seen. The panic evaporated when she saw who was walking towards her and a small smile broke out on her face. It was a group of police officers, flanked by someone in the familiar blue uniform of Hoddington Manor.

"Officers, thank goodness," she started before she saw their pistols, pointing directly towards Daniel's chest.

"No!" she cried, realising how they were viewing this scene. "Don't hurt him."

She pulled his injured body closer to her own, trying to get in front of him but he kept shifting so she wouldn't be in the line of fire.

The officers ran forwards. They moved around her, forcing Daniel's face into the mud. He howled in agony as they wrenched his injured arm, pulling it behind his back. A boot came down on his head to keep him on the ground.

"No – please." Annabel begged, still on her knees, the panic re-surfacing to a dangerous level.

One of the bigger officers bent down as she started clawing at them in desperation. Grabbing her shoulders he pulled her back and into the air. She kicked out her legs, letting out an ear piercing yell.

"DANIEL!" she screamed over and over again. "Let him go!"

She began to sob as they hauled Daniel to his feet with another cry of pain. The officers caught him roughly, throwing him onto the back of a small trap sitting in a slightly clearer area of the woods. The trees in its path had all been recently cut down, to form something of a road. The officer released his hold on Annabel.

"It's okay miss." He bowed his head slightly. "You're safe now."

Chapter Eighteen

Annabel heard Daniel call after her as the trap jerked into action.

"I'm so sorry," she sobbed in his direction. She could see the frown in between his eyes and the hard line of his mouth as he tried unsuccessfully to reassure her.

"I love you."

She saw his lips move over the words but couldn't hear them uttered. The trap disappeared into the trees before she had the time to respond.

"Why - why are you doing this?" she sobbed.

"We were ordered by your father to bring in the man you were found with. It's over now Miss." There was feigned loyalty in his voice.

"I can take you to the real kidnapper. I know where he is...please."

"No Miss, we have to get you home."

"NO! Let him go! I – I order you to let him go! LISTEN TO ME!"

She heard the officer laugh as she pummelled his chest. He lifted her with ease onto the back of his horse and kicked it as hard as he could. Annabel wanted to jump down but they were now galloping through the woods at break neck speed, such an endeavour would have been suicide.

After a while she gave up fighting. These men had said they were taking her home. Her father would surely sort out the misunderstanding in a matter of seconds.

"Look Ma'am," said the sergeant, breaking through the heavy silence as they slowed to a gentle trot about half an hour later. There was no trace of amusement or enthusiasm in his voice. "You were kidnapped, believed murdered, we were told – and paid handsomely for it - to get you back and arrest the man that took you. We're just doing our job."

Annabel saw it all now; they needed a scapegoat to get their money. Going to the village would take them another few days. Why would they bother when they could just blame Daniel and save themselves the work? Annabel spit in the officers face, he laughed in hers.

"Well I can see all the hype surrounding you was wrong, you're not much more than a peasant. I'm sure your fiancé will be very excited to get you back. "

"You must have forgotten your place officer. I will ruin you!"

He laughed again and seized up her wrists with one hand, holding them firmly around his waist. The experience of riding with the officer was completely different to riding with Daniel. This man's flesh was softer with too many rich meals. His uniform scratched her face as it bounced against his shoulder. Daniel's carving dug painfully into the skin just above her heart.

Annabel must have imagined her homecoming thousands of times over the past few weeks. In all of those fantasies she had been seated in one of her family's fancy carriages, dressed from head to toe in silk and jewels with Billy, Jen, Patsy and Daniel at her side.

This was as far from that daydream as possible.

The officer let go of her hands as they reached the edge of the forest, emerging into a sudden burst of morning sun shine that made Annabel squint. The journey back had been significantly shorter than the journey there, suggesting Trevor hadn't really known where he was going, or had ridden for much shorter bursts of the day.

The officer made her jump off the horse and remount so she was sitting side saddle.

"As befits a lady of your station, of course," he remarked, his voice dripping with sarcasm.

Annabel tried to rearrange the ratty trousers and ripped dress that she had on so she at least resembled the former queen of high society but gave up almost immediately, seeing the effort was futile. The officer, back on the horse as well, combed his fat fingers through her tangled hair, pulling loose a few strands on several occasions.

It was an ironic twist that, in that moment, she felt exactly the same as when she had been taken...vulnerable and violated.

However, just before they were about to turn towards the centre of town the officer seemed to change his mind and led her, not towards Hoddington Manor, but towards the police station.

It being a clear day, Annabel spotted the big house seated on a large, steep hill off to their right and got a sudden thrill of anticipation.

They made it to the station within ten minutes. Annabel could already see the trap that had taken Daniel parked outside and she looked around frantically for some sign of him. There was none.

The officer, who was still yet to identify himself, jumped off the horse with a thud, as his considerable bulk hit the floor and pulled her after him. They bypassed the main entrance, raised above the street by three granite steps, choosing instead a small back door. Annabel was led down a dingy corridor lined with five or six closed doors, each holding the name of a sergeant, before they reached one that read 'Sergeant T. Link' and entered. As they crossed the threshold the floorboards squeaked beneath Annabel's feet. She immediately rounded on the officer.

"You have to free Daniel."

The officer laughed. "I'll leave your father to decide that one."

"But he is innocent and you are supposed to bring about justice."

The officer gave another hollow laugh. "Yeah, sure we are sweet pea. We are supposed to feed our families as well. That's what I'm doing. Wait here."

He pointed to a low, wooden chair on the far side of a rickety desk and closed the door behind him. Annabel could hear his heavy footfalls echo down the hall.

Finally alone, Annabel seized her chance and dashed out the door. She heard it click back into place and closed her eyes briefly, hoping the officer had not heard it.

She had to speak to her father.

As quietly as she could, Annabel ran along the hall towards the door at the end. When she reached it she darted outside and ran along the cobbled street, her bare feet slapping against the smooth stones.

She thrust her arm out when she saw a cab roll past but it didn't stop. Annabel cursed under her breath and continued along at a steady jog, receiving many disgusted looks along the way as she fled into the more upmarket part of town. People crossed the road when they saw her coming, too caught up in their own selfishness to look past the ragged clothes and see one of the wealthiest women in the world, in desperate need of assistance.

As she started up the hill that would inevitably lead her home, a couple of people got up the nerve to stop her, or try to, but Annabel shook them all off. She continued now at a faster pace, until she reached the top with burning lungs and searing limbs. With the manor now in full sight Annabel felt a touch of her old vanity creep back into her blood so she reached into her bodice, pulling out the hair comb which she twisted into her limp, greasy hair. She hoped she would be recognised just enough to allow her through the gates. She smoothed her torn dress down with her hands, noticing how much rougher they looked, the skin now dry and red, before glancing up.

Looking upon the manor, Annabel realised she had never truly appreciated the grandeur of the place. She had called the building home for eighteen years but had never even looked at it until then, as she stood as just another spectator to the Hoddingtons' unachievable perfection.

Taking a deep breath she quickly reached the set of gigantic, golden gates that shielded the world from the splendour they couldn't afford, whilst simultaneously trapping the wealthy family inside.

Beyond the gleaming gates the walls of Hoddington Manor shone pure white. Hundreds of windows studded the surface, glistening in the dull sunlight like row upon row of shimmering diamonds, set against the majestic pallor of royal skin. White roses crept along the numerous pillars flanking the grand entrance, in such a way that proved dozens of gardeners spent entire days pruning them. The grounds around its walls were immaculate, dotted with impressive sculptures and fountains arranged with hundreds more carefully tended white flowers. These grounds stood in stark contrast to the acres of unruly meadows beyond them, used throughout the summer for hunting. Just on the other side of the gate was a small, one story house resided in by the team of uniformed gatekeepers.

This was probably the only time Annabel had ever looked upon her home with anything longer than a fleeting glance and she was in awe.

She stood on the wrong side of these gates for about five minutes, her hands wrapped around the golden bars in an attempt to see how she was supposed to enter on foot. The gates had always been opened as she approached before so she did not know the protocol when they were closed.

A young girl in a black maid's uniform passed her with a basket of fragrant, fresh herbs and made her way around to the smaller, servant's entrance where a guard stood on the opposite side. Neither of them paid the beggar in rags so much as a look.

Annabel took her lead and followed the unsuspecting woman. The maid quickened her step, realising within seconds she was being followed. The guard slammed the gate behind the maid with such finality it shook for a good few seconds afterwards. Annabel, hearing hooves falling gently behind her, glanced over her shoulder. Just crossing over the brow of the hill was the officer, Sergeant Link she assumed, remembering the sign on his door. He was closing in on her rapidly.

"Um...hello, I um -" She began talking to the guard in a hurried voice, her mind fogged by exhaustion, her lungs still clamouring for breath. The guard studiously ignored her, his arms pressed to his sides, his body motionless.

"Excuse me, guard. I need to get through to my house. Excuse me...I ORDER YOU TO LISTEN TO ME!"

The guard flinched at her authoritative tone and his eyes flickered to her face. It was the only part of him that moved. They widened as they caught sight of the glittering hair comb and then sunk into thin slits as if he was disbelieving his own vision. He seemed to be thinking very hard.

"As you are wondering, yes my name is Miss Annabel Maria Hoddington. I live here, please let me through."

She employed her trademark air of impatience to make her case more believable. She clearly succeeded for the gatekeeper gasped. His eyes flickered back to the diamonds in her hair. They seemed to offer him the proof he was desperately seeking and his hands flew up to his mouth. The expression of his shock was so great and unexpected he swayed on his feet for a few seconds, as if he would topple over. He looked hurriedly around for someone to tell him what to do. When he found no one, he swallowed, his adams apple bobbing in his throat.

"Miss – Miss Hoddington."

The man sank into a low bow and then jumped, as if remembering for the first time the large gate standing between them. He immediately searched through his pockets, drawing out a large ring of keys that jangled in his trembling hand. Fumbling through them he eventually found the correct one and opened the small gate, embedded inside the larger. As she stepped through it, he bowed again and offered her his white gloved hand for assistance. She must have looked as tired as she felt. His crumpled expression as she passed him told her she didn't smell too great either.

"I have been absent for quite some time and getting home in a prompt manner would be most satisfying," Annabel said.

The guard nodded frantically, looking around himself again for someone to help him. He seemed torn between

escorting his mistress to the house and staying at his ordered post.

"It is quite alright," Annabel continued, noticing his in-
ternal struggle. "I can escort myself home and a sufficient
bonus will find its way into your wages. Thank you. Oh
and tell the officer behind me, my family are incredibly
grateful for my safe return and they will happily provide
him with a light lunch, should he wish to head around to
the servant's kitchen."

She smirked up at the officer who had just pulled up by
the gate, his mouth hanging open at her insult. She waved
before turning on her heel towards home.

"No!" she heard Sergeant Link exclaim in an outraged
tone.

This situation being a much more familiar one the
guard began his spiel, repeating a speech that was clearly used on all unwanted visitors, with an air of detached
disinterest.

"I am to take her into the house," Annabel heard the
officer plead somewhat pathetically, his authority failing
him. The gatekeeper repeated the exact same speech, obviously bored.

"That is quite unnecessary, I assure you." Annabel
called over her shoulder. "You see I have my own legs
that work perfectly fine."

She heard the gatekeeper's muffled snigger, as if he
had raised a hand to his mouth to hide the expression and
she winked at him. He seemed taken aback by his young
mistress's friendliness but quickly reassembled his impas-

sive facial expression.

Annabel employed her usual upper class tone. It felt strange now on her out of practice tongue.

"I believe your duty was to return me safely to my house officer, nothing more. You have therefore fulfilled your brief. If you wish to stay, as I said earlier, by all means you may wait out here with the rest of the staff. I would extend you my thanks but frankly, it would be a lie. Good day."

Sergeant Link's face fell into a vicious glare and Annabel smiled back at him as she walked further up the immaculate drive.

Annabel had quite forgotten the magnitude of her home. Having survived in nothing more than a stable, the sheer size of this house seemed excessive to say the least.

As she reached the entrance, time seemed to slow down.

Stepping inside the grand foyer, her bare feet slapping against the marble, Annabel was surrounded by the perfumed scents of her illustrious childhood. There were gasps from all angles as the various members of staff caught sight of her, stopping in their tasks to register the girl silhouetted majestically in the door.

One gasp in particular caught Annabel's attention more than all the others. A tall woman, dressed from head to toe in black silk, had stopped in the middle of the floor, her hand clutching her chest in shock.

Annabel approached her mother slowly, as if unsure she was truly there. The elder woman had the exact same expression on her own, gaunt face. When they were within a few inches of each other she reached out, brushing Annabel's cheek with cold fingers. She drew in a shaky breath and did something that took her daughter (already on the edge of a meltdown) by total surprise; she drew her into her embrace, cradling her head against her breast as both of them collapsed onto the floor in a pool of black silk.

Annabel breathed in the expensive smell of her mother's skin whilst the beautiful material of her tailored dress caressed her touch. Annabel sat as still as possible in the embrace of someone who she believed could keep her safe, terrified that should she move too quickly, she would wake up back in the stable.

An unknown amount of time passed as the two women sat on the gleaming floor. Servants wiped their eyes at the emotional scene they had witnessed, before moving off down the many different corridors to discreetly continue their chores elsewhere. Lady Elizabeth pulled back slightly, holding Annabel's chin in one hand as she turned her face this way and that to look at it from every available angle.

"I hope no one saw you looking like this," she tutted.

Annabel found this disapproving person far more familiar to her than the motherly, sensitive woman of a few seconds ago. She noticed lines had appeared around her mother's mouth and eyes, as if from worry.

"Yes Mother," she replied, her voice thick.

"Right." Rearranging her face to one of complete composure and erecting herself with her former posture, Lady Elizabeth pulled Annabel up beside her, patting her hand absentmindedly. "I must contact your father at once and you must dress for luncheon. I'm sure you are quite exhausted but we must keep up appearances and your father would worry terribly if he saw you like this. You're too thin Annabel, it doesn't suit you."

She rang a bell off to the left of her and bent forwards as if to kiss her daughter on the forehead. Just before her lips brushed the skin, she stopped and pulled back, wrinkling her nose. Annabel stepped away from her, embarrassed.

Stepping back as well, with one last smile for her daughter, a smile radiating through her entire face, she turned and walked up the stairs. Annabel was escorted up the opposite set of stairs, a maid appearing as if from thin air to escort her.

Annabel put one foot in front of the other in a trance, her limbs felt heavy and stiff from weariness and her skin tingled with the promise of an imminent bath. With her guard down her thoughts quickly fled back to Daniel, Patsy, Billy and Genevieve, wondering what could be happening to them at that moment. Hearing a rustle behind her Annabel glanced back, noticing another maid following her, sweeping the mud she was treading into the carpet. Annabel stopped.

"I'm sorry," she whispered, bending down to help.

"It – it's okay Miss," said the second maid, glancing uncertainly towards the first. They exchanged a glance. Annabel had never spoken to a maid before.

"P-please you've – you need to dress for lunch," the maid stammered. She touched Annabel's arm thus stopping her from helping. "P-please Miss."

"Oh...okay." She stood up, stumbling along the richly carpeted corridor.

She noticed more maids and footmen all staring as she walked past, too shocked to bow or curtsey. They were looking down at Annabel's bare feet, running up her body to the tattered clothes and tangled hair. She had never noticed how many members of staff there were at the house and suddenly, an idea hit her. She turned around racing down the stairs after her mother, using a stock of energy she hadn't thought she possessed.

"Mother – Mother!" she called, running up the west wing stairs and barging into the burgundy walled writing room that belonged to her mother. The elder woman was sitting behind a highly polished oak desk with her back to a floor to ceiling window, accessorised with red and gold edged curtains. Her head jerked up at the sound of her daughter's voice and she jumped to her feet.

"Annabel! Why are you not – you were going to get dressed."

"Yes." She looked down at her horrible clothes and bare feet. "I will but first, the place I escaped...the village I was taken to -"

She broke off, remembering her mother knew nothing of the last few weeks of her life. She waved a hand in front of her dismissively. "I'll explain it all after lunch, or at lunch – whichever. Well, I escaped with some friends that helped me while I was there -"

"Annabel, please. You're over exciting yourself."

"Listen Mother! Please. When the police shot Daniel – I need to talk to father the second he gets in because he is innocent, and what is happening to him is barbaric – but there were two people and a baby, their horse bolted."

"Annabel let's discuss this -"

"Later? No. In fact, whilst you're writing to father write to the station, Daniel needs to come to dinner tonight, I simply cannot have him sitting in a prison cell. Patsy, Billy and Genevieve, they need to be found and brought here, they could live in the house. In my wing of course. Billy's amazing with horses, I'm sure he would help out. People have been pretending to be relations for years, we will just say they are cousins and be done with it. The staff, if they dispersed around town, we could find them in a matter of minutes."

Her mother looked at her as if she were deranged. She walked over to her, a scared look on her face. It was as if she were approaching a horse that could bolt at any moment.

"Annabel you've clearly had an ordeal, you're in shock. Please just go and change."

Tears of anger fell from Annabel's eyes.

"Are you really that heartless? Daniel can't stay in prison! I don't even know what happened to the others. They are the reason I am still alive Mother-"

"Don't – don't say things like that Annabel."

"It's the truth. Please help them. For my sake, help

them."

"I'll do what I can child but you must dress before your father arrives." She fingered the course fabric of Annabel's ripped dress. "Make sure the maids burn this thing, it's beyond vile."

Annabel smiled slightly but without much humour.

"Yes Mother. Please talk to Father before I come down, he must free Daniel and we must find the others."

"I'm sure he'll do everything he can," she looked slightly to the right of Annabel, towards a maid who had run in after her.

"Take her to her room, she must bathe. And make sure she rests before you bring her down to luncheon, she is quite beside herself."

Patting Annabel's cheek in a slightly disinterested way she walked past her - wiping her hand as she did so - and placed the letter she had composed into a crisp envelope. "And see to it that Lord Hoddington gets this within the hour."

"Yes Ma'am."

The maid gave a little curtsey, taking the letter and passing it to a nearby footman, leading Annabel once more up into the east wing.

Annabel walked up the stairs with a feeling of foreboding. It was almost as if she were walking towards her own prison, somewhere she would be polished and pruned, ready to be placed back on display as soon as possible. Her parents' best business asset had returned and it seemed they were anxious to forget the past few weeks had even occurred.

Once in her old bedroom Annabel glanced around, taking in the familiar sights. The Fleur-de-lis patterned wallpaper was still exactly as it had been when she left, matching the gold colour of the curtains draping around the tall window and queen-sized bed.

As Annabel walked further into her past, she ran her fingers lightly over the mantel of an elaborately carved marble fireplace that still smelt faintly of smoke, although it had been freshly laid at least a dozen times since she had been gone.

Breathing in the expensive smells she had grown up with, Annabel continued slowly towards the window. Peering out over the distant forest she stretched her hand towards it, thinking of Daniel's tender touch on her skin. Her fingers found only the cold glass which fogged beneath her touch, leaving a ghostly imprint when her arm fell back to her side.

"Your bath is ready Miss."

Annabel jumped, startled out of her daze and made her way into the adjoining room. It was a strange feeling being back in these walls. The rooms hadn't changed since she was last there. She could even still smell the perfume she had worn that final morning.

She stepped off the soft carpet and onto the heated tiles in the bathroom. The fire was raging in the fireplace, filling her with a kind of warmth she hadn't felt in weeks.

Tugging the ill-fitting clothes off she heard a distant clatter and looked down, jumping as she stared directly into Daniel's eyes, forever immortalised in his craftsmanship. Annabel bent slowly and walked back into her bedroom, as if in a trance, where she placed the carving in her bedside cabinet. When she reappeared in the bathroom the maids ceased their conversation immediately. Two maids rushed forwards with a warm cloth, cleaning off the worst of the mud and grime from Annabel's feet and legs before she was asked to step into the steaming water. She entered the bath tub slowly. Her skin, now unused to such luxuries as hot water, turned red as soon as it hit the water. Once she was fully immersed Annabel sighed as the warmth crept into her aches, soothing them almost instantly. She hadn't realised just how fatigued she was until the water began seeping into her muscles. She felt the dirt and sweat slide out from her pores as perfumed soap was lathered into her skin and hair.

As Annabel sat there, the maids worked. They rinsed her hair and brushed her teeth until they felt as soft beneath her tongue as polished pearls. Following this her rough hands and feet were scrubbed and filed to within an inch of their lives, her nails clipped and polished until they once more sat even and shining. They were restoring her to her former self, pristine and perfect on the outside yet they couldn't fix the wounds that had mauled her soul.

She could hear the maids whispering to each other somewhere in her subconscious but she didn't pay attention. For the first time in her life she didn't care what people were saying about her.

After the initial scrubbing Annabel was told to step out

whilst the now black water was emptied and fresh water replaced it. This was done three times before eventually she was deemed clean enough and dried off. Whilst the three maids continued to work, rubbing oils and lotions into her skin and dabbing perfume behind her ears, some other maids spent the time in Annabel's large closet, altering the outfit they wanted her to wear so it fit her newly shrunken frame. They settled on a high necked dress overlain with lace ruffles and small pearl buttons.

A thin white chemise was pulled over her head before being layered up with undergarments and petticoats. Finally, she was laced into a corset and her arms pulled into a pink silk robe that trailed the floor as she shuffled in her stocking clad feet to the dressing table. Annabel looked into the mirror, watching as her team brushed out her tangled hair, cutting off the ends with a practiced precision so it fell once more in delicate waves down her back, gleaming celestially in the crystal light above their heads. Her face was still porcelain in both appearance and touch. Fingers slid into her hair, working it up into an elaborate bun at the nape of her neck. They slid a new hair comb into the bun, adorned with a further cluster of pearls.

When this was done, the maids fixing Annabel's appearance crept into the closet. She could hear a hushed up argument before one of them returned. The dress was clearly not ready and the maids were scared.

"P-perhaps you would care for a rest Miss?" one of them stuttered.

"Yes, I think I should like that." Annabel tried to smile

but the emotion never made it onto her face. Looking away she walked back into her room, taking a well stuffed pillow off of her bed and sitting herself on her deep window seat, she looked out once more at the forest in the distance.

She fingered the lace at the edge of her robe, watching the light shine off the silk as it tumbled down over the sill and onto the floor. She placed one foot on the carpet, marvelling at how soft it was even through her stocking. Once more, she wondered how she could have failed to notice how fantastically made every part of this estate was. Her family owned nearly every one of the houses in and around the village, as well as several estates around the country.

Looking back out over the forest Annabel's thoughts quickly flew to Daniel, suffering unknown terror and pain as she sat in the height of luxury.

A maid placed a cup of tea with lemon and sugar on a small table by her feet and she sipped at it absentmindedly, the hot liquid burning her throat as it slid into her empty stomach. She hadn't realised how thirsty she was until that point. Pouring another from the gold tea pot she cradled it in her hands as tears slid silently down her cheeks.

She must have fallen asleep for she didn't notice the maid coming up behind her until she was tapped gently on the shoulder. She shot to her feet, startled, fixing her eyes on the young girl in a neatly pressed black gown and white apron.

"Miss? Your father has arrived home and is anxious to

see you. He said he will wait in the family parlour."

"Yes, yes of course. Thank you."

She set down her now empty tea cup and made her way back into the dressing room, throwing her robe onto the chaise. Behind a hand painted screen more maids helped her into her now smaller clothes. They didn't fit as well as they would have before she left but they were close enough. She glanced down at her beaded shoes and then up into the full length mirror, gasping as the reflection of her former self gazed out at her. Pinching her cheeks she took a deep breath, suddenly nervous and walked out of the room, towards the smallest of the parlours downstairs.

The expensive material around her legs rustled as she walked, her heels clicking on the floor. She tried to take a deep breath but her corset was pulled too tight, making anything more than half a lung impossible. The palms of her hands had turned cold, although sweat was making them damp. The bodice of her dress jumped as her heart hammered against her ribs.

Inside the parlour, her father was stood looking into the fire, his newly lined forehead creased up in stress. One hand rested on his hip, the other on the mantel piece. Her mother was sat in a large wing backed chair still wearing her black mourning gown. Hearing the soft clicking of Annabel's step Lord Hoddington turned around. He strode over to his daughter with a fierce desperation in his eyes and seized her in an out of character hug. The embrace was so tight she couldn't breathe but she clung to the back of his tailored suit, equally as desperate for her father's touch. He kissed her cheek, his wispy beard brushing across her face. It was such a familiar feeling that Annabel's eyes grew hot, her throat tightening.

"Let her breathe Grayson," her mother ordered in a firm voice but she was grinning insanely. Her fingers fidgeted as she clasped and unclasped them in her lap. Annabel took her father's hand, unwilling to let go of him and sat between her parents. They sat like that until a uniformed butler came in, announcing lunch and asking them to adjourn to the family dining room. This was the least elaborate and smallest of the dining rooms, one where they could all sit closer to one another and perhaps discuss Annabel's disappearance.

They walked to dinner in silence, Grayson Hoddington's hand in Annabel's, her second arm hooked around her mother's elbow. On the table was a spread of all Annabel's favourite foods. There were six courses in total. Caviar was followed by salmon tartlets, a steaming bowl of brown Windsor soup came before ornately modelled ice cream sculptures in the shape of birds, in various bright colours, to cleanse their palettes. Following this they ate stuffed pheasant, finishing with a moist sponge cake, the icing made from fresh strawberries. Annabel stuffed herself until she thought she might burst, using all of her will power to eat somewhat daintily, with the manners she was brought up with and not to just grab fistfuls of food. However, her hunger overtook her a few times and she thought she noticed her mother glancing at her uncertainly from across the table.

After they ate they moved into the conservatory. Here, surrounded by sweet smelling roses, freshly cut from the garden and arranged expertly in large antique vases, Annabel tried as best as she could to explain everything that had happened to her. Having thought about her tale before she told it, she left out the worst of the abuse that befell her, to make for a more watered down version of events.

She told them she had been knocked out, that she had woken up in a small village deep within the woods and stayed in a stable with Billy. She explained about Patsy, bringing her home comforts and food whilst trying her best to tell them about the kindness of Daniel, how he had gotten himself beaten up and she had nursed him back to health, hoping this would make them proud of their daughter. Looking up she noticed her father standing across the room looking stony faced.

"So this Daniel is a thug?"

"No! No! He was protecting his mother! He is a kind man Father. He helped me, he brought us food and – and friendship."

"Just friendship?"

She blushed and her father nodded knowingly, his facial expression growing angrier by the second.

"Did you forget that we have secured for you the most eligible young man in the country, if not the world?"

"Father that was not the point of me telling you this. I've thanked you for my engagement so many times but things have changed. I have changed. How do I even know that he still wants to marry me? I've never even met him."

She hadn't planned on this particular turn in the conversation happening so soon. She had only hoped to free Daniel and figure out the rest afterwards.

"He arrived here not two hours after you left. Punctual on top of everything else. You will marry him Annabel. Think of someone other than yourself for once."

Her mouth fell open in shock.

"How dare you! I've done nothing but think of you the entire time I was away. This isn't about me, it's Daniel-"

"Who is an abusive thief from what you've told me-"

"NO! Father please, we can talk about all this later, just release him. He doesn't deserve any of this! He has suffered so much his entire life, don't make him suffer more."

"He will stay exactly where he is. I've spoken to the police already and he is going on trial next week. They've already been paid my child, it's too late."

She wrapped her arms around her waist trying to hold herself together as she fell back into her chair, her breath coming fast once more.

"Father please," she whispered. "I'll do whatever you want. Just please don't condemn him because of me."

"I won't risk the improvement of our family, improvements I have worked for my entire life, by letting you indulge yourself in childish lust. By letting you lower yourself to a relationship with an impoverished, violent boy. You will ruin all of our reputations. He will not leave that prison. I will make him as comfortable as I can but I can't risk this engagement."

Annabel straightened up in a rage.

"I won't marry Theodore until you release Daniel! I won't do it!"

Her voice was high pitched and shrill. At the sound of it her father shot to his feet, one hand on each arm of her chair, pushing her back against the cushions. His face was less than an inch from his daughters.

"You don't marry him young lady and you can never again call yourself my daughter."

Annabel shrank back further as her mother let out a sob, her hands going to her flushed throat.

"Grayson, you can't."

"I can do whatever the hell I like in my own house! Don't undermine my position!"

Annabel's eyes glistened with tears. She had been let down by the person who was supposed to protect her above all others, simply indulging in his own selfish ideas of higher power and riches he already had a sickening amount of.

"Please Father, help him. I can't survive if he's not happy."

He took her chin in his fat fingers, forcing her to look at him. Her tears fell onto his thumb.

"I won't do it. There's things even I can't influence. The police have been after his family for more years than you've been alive. There was nothing I could do with all the money in the world, even if I'd wanted to. You haven't condemned him dear, his name condemned him."

She could barely speak for crying.

"B-but surely there must be – there must be something. He's innocent, why won't you see that? H-his brother and father they - they are the ones you want, I know where they are."

Frantically she leapt to her feet and ran to the door, pushing her father out of the way in her haste.

"I'll take – I'll take you there now. Please, Father."

She halted, tears racing down her cheeks with one hand on the door handle. Her father closed his eyes in exasperation.

"I'm sorry Annabel."

And with that he got up, straightening his suit. Turning to the footman by the fire he said, "have the carriage brought around to the front," before brushing past his daughter into the entrance hall.

"No!" Annabel sobbed, chasing after him. "FATHER! LISTEN TO ME!"

Her mother grabbed Annabel's arm, clinging on with surprising strength. Annabel tried desperately to get away from her grasp but she hadn't enough energy left in her body and tripped over her own heel, falling to the floor in a heap of ridiculous lace.

"Mother please. I need him," she sobbed quietly.

Lady Elizabeth brought her face close to Annabel's ear.

"You see what this boy has done to you already? He has driven you mad! Do you think I married for love Annabel? You think these childish notions got me where I am today? I married for prospects, for the best life in which to raise a family, best life for you. Love is a brilliant fantasy but it's not real. What you're feeling now will fade and when it does you're left with only a lifetime of regret. Theodore is a good match for you. He is a kind man and he has fortune Annabel. He can raise you to heights you've only ever dreamed of. You have to let this boy go. I will see to it as well that he stays in that prison."

She stood sharply and strode out of the room, her posture perfectly erect, leaving her newly returned daughter alone.

Annabel sat for hours huddled as much as her corset would allow whilst the conservatory grew colder, leaving only when her stomach turned violently and she rushed to the nearest vase, throwing up noisily. She felt a sense of exultation as she did so, knowing it was one of her father's favourite ornaments.

She made her way to her room, being sick in two separate bathrooms on the way. Her body was already rejecting the large quantities of rich food she had just consumed. Three maids stood from the chaise at Annabel's entrance, rushing over to her as she bent over the chamber pot and threw up once more. Wiping her mouth one maid swiped the pot out of the room before the smell could infiltrate the perfumed air. Annabel padded into her bedroom, ripping off her tailored clothes as she went and dropping them behind her like bread crumbs. She let the maids unlace her corset and slip a thin nightgown over her head. The first maid came back in with a large jug of water and a crystal glass, a small bottle of medicine beside it. It was sickly sweet, the liquid so thick it stuck to the walls of her throat.

Collapsing against the plumped up pillows, her heart ached thinking of the situation Daniel, Billy, Patsy and Genevieve could be in at that very minute, whilst she sat here. She felt useless and betrayed. Rolling onto her side she succumbed to tears once more.

Chapter Nineteen

Sleep was hard to come by that first night. Despite her exhaustion, nightmares of her friends, her love and her ghastly experiences of the past few weeks haunted her dreams until she woke, sweating and nauseous.

Looking up in the darkness, her brow shining with sweat, she reached for the glass of water. Tasting the foul, acrid taste of vomit on her tongue she tried to wash it away with the cool liquid. As she set it back down her fingers brushed the bottle of medicine. Tightening her grip around it she eased herself into a seated position, running her eyes over the small label, her hands trembling. The maids wouldn't disturb her much before midday so long as she didn't ring the bell. She could drink just enough to knock herself out until then. Perhaps with enough sleep, she could reason with her father more effectively. She thought again of Daniel in a cold, damp cell, the picture becoming more gruesome with every moment she sat there. Next she thought of her father, telling her she must marry the man she didn't love and the mapped out future stretching in front of her. There was no way out. Her exhausted mind clouded over, she felt utterly trapped and miserable. The pain in her gut only intensified her guilt.

Daniel was in this position because of her. Patsy, Billy and Genevieve were facing unknown horror, because of her. Still shaking, she uncorked the bottle. Raising it to her lips she took a single deep breath, tilting it into her mouth. The sickly sweet medicine coated her tongue as the image of Daniel's face shot into her mind so vividly she cried out in shock. She spluttered as the liquid hit the back of her throat, gagging and coughing until the sheets were covered in bile and medicine in the instinctual fight for breath. In frustration she let out a scream, throwing the bottle at the fireplace where it smashed, chipping the marble. The remaining liquid dripped down slowly into the hearth where it sizzled on the still hot embers, releasing a bitter smell of burning into the room. A maid, who must have been sitting right outside the door, came running in, registering the small shards of glass scattered across the carpet and the liquid dripping from Annabel's mouth.

"Miss!" She ran over, wiping her mistress's mouth with a damp cloth as Annabel continued to cry out in anguish, clawing at the soiled sheets. The young girl rang the bell fixed to the wall, summoning more maids who arrived still in their night clothes.

"Call a doctor," the first maid shouted.

"No, please...no!" Annabel tried to protest but it was futile.

The sheets were quickly stripped from around Annabel's trembling body and changed for clean, freshly ironed ones of almost identical colour and pattern. Every trace of the broken bottle from the floor was cleared away in seconds. Once she was settled again the few gulps of medicine she had managed to swallow, teamed with the past few week's mainly sleepless nights, caused her eyelids to turn leaden, but still she couldn't sleep.

The doctor arrived just an hour later, his suit crumpled as if it had been hastily thrown on. Annabel only half registered the cold hands on her skin and the needle entering a vein in the crook of her arm.

"This will put her to sleep for about eight hours," he croaked, close to her ear. He sounded like an elderly man. "She has endured a very trying ordeal, so she will need a few weeks bed rest to properly heal. She is clearly quite distressed."

Annabel's mind grew foggy as the medicine worked its way into her blood stream, making her muscles heavy and her limbs uncontrollable. Finally, everything went black.

The sedative in her veins took a long time to wear off. Annabel was first aware of a gentle breeze caressing her skin and she smiled thinking of Daniel and the night beside the stream. Her finger twitched as she moved her hand towards her love but, instead of meeting the warm comfort of Daniel, her fingers took purchase on a feather stuffed pillow. Her eyes fluttered open, taking in her expensive surroundings.

Annabel sat bolt upright. Her head spun as her stomach lurched. She swallowed, waiting for her vision to come back then lowered her feet onto the soft carpet and stood up, swaying for several seconds before she was able to take a step forwards.

Eventually finding her way into her bathroom she splashed her face with ice cold water, somewhat waking herself up. In her closet she pulled out the first clothes she came across, fighting for several minutes with the hooks on the front of her corset.

She stumbled as she stepped into her stockings, ripping three before she eventually succeeded in placing a pair on her legs. Her pale pink dress, the garment having been freshly sewn and hung up that evening, was easier to assemble. It took an hour in total for her to dress herself. The medicine still clogged her mind, making her movements slow and fuzzy. She twisted her hair up simply, shoving a hat on her head to cover the poor craftsmanship before stumbling out of the door and down the stairs as quickly as possible, without appearing improper and thus attracting attention.

She tiptoed down the stairs as quietly as she could, choosing not to take the back stairs as there would surely be hundreds of servants through those passages. The foyer, thankfully, was empty so she fled across the polished floor, skidding out of the entrance and into the blinding sun.

"Annabel, stop this instance."

Annabel squeezed her eyes shut in exasperation.

"No Mother, you don't control me," she slurred, her tongue still numb in her mouth from the sedative.

The elder woman grabbed Annabel's arm, her nails digging into her daughter's skin through the thin material of her dress.

"You will not take one more step out of this house young lady. I refuse to let you destroy everything we have built up for one ridiculous infatuation."

"I don't care what you want. This is my life. I love him Mother."

"You don't know the first thing about love. This is not love my child, love is providing for your family. That thug cannot give you anything."

"He can give me happiness. How can you deny me that?"

"Theodore will provide you with everything you need."

"You cannot condemn an innocent man!"

"It has already been done."

Annabel's face fell, her eyes roamed over her mother's stern face for some signs of false truth.

"No. You wouldn't."

"He is to be sentenced without trial. Your father has already signed the paperwork Annabel, the money changed hands last night. I will not let that boy's hold on you risk my - our, bright future. My family's fate will not be left to chance Annabel, that boy will not marry you. You will do as you're told and you will marry Theodore."

"You - you witch. I hope you rot in hell!"

With that her mother let go of Annabel's arm. Annabel stumbled backwards, out into the sun. The second she made it outside another, colder hand grabbed her shoulder.

"No Miss, you are under doctor's orders to stay inside. You have had quite the upset, you mustn't over exert yourself."

Annabel clawed at the man's white coat, trying desperately to break free. She screamed like she was deranged. Once she was restrained a sharp pain entered her neck and her limbs grew sluggish. As the medicine burnt its way into her veins her vision faded.

"I'm sorry my child but it's for the best. I'm only thinking of your future."

Chapter Twenty

Annabel spent the rest of that day in and out of consciousness, her body unresponsive to even the simplest of movements.

When she finally woke the room was swathed in darkness and she was alone.

Looking around her she noticed the window was still slightly ajar, letting in a cool breeze. The oil lamp was turned on low. The light glinted off of a silver tray housing dry bread and water.

Annabel turned her face away from the sustenance. If her parents were going to play this game, she would play it right back.

Shifting until she was in a seated position Annabel pulled open the drawer in her bedside cabinet. Removing the carving she cradled it in her palm, tip toeing to the window seat where she sat amongst the cushions, tracing her fingertip over Daniel's tiny features. She imagined him sat beside her, his warm breath on her face, his earthy smell surrounding her completely.

She figured she must have fallen asleep for the sound of the wind, bending the trees into dangerous angles in the forest, snapped Annabel back to consciousness. It must have been early morning as there was a dim light attempting to force its way through the heavy clouds. Torrential rain now hammered down whilst her curtains ballooned into the bedroom. The window was smacking rhythmically into the wall as the wind blew it off the latch. Annabel jumped up and forced the window into place. She stepped back, her entire body shivering.

"Nice night ain't it."

Annabel's heart stopped.

"Knew you'd forget 'bout the idiots soon as you got 'ome."

His voice was more steady than usual, the smell of liquor not quite as strong. Whirling around Annabel came face to face with Tom.

Rain dripped off of his scraggily hair and beard, leaving muddy marks on the cream carpet. His face was set into the hard expression of rage.

"Ya think you could jus' run away an' I'd not find ya? You're stupider than I thought."

Annabel didn't say a word, her mind had gone blank and nothing in this useless room of finery would make so much a cut on him. The oil lamp was the only thing of substance but that would surely burn down the whole house.

She staggered back, her body still trembling.

"I - I have maids right outside my door. You won't be able to lay so much a finger on me without being arrested."

Tom laughed but the sound was anything but pleasant. His lips sneered, whilst the laughter came out dull and menacing.

"I've checked, stupid! It's jus' you and me, all alone."

The room was suddenly illuminated as a bolt of lightning pulsed through the air, quickly followed by a deep rumble of thunder. The lightning glinted off the golden rope beside Annabel's bed which was attached to a wall of bells in the kitchen. She dived to the side, catching hold of it just before Tom grabbed her from behind. In the far distance the bell jangled at her touch, Tom growled. He let go of her, smashing his fist into the side of her face. Her mouth filled with the coppery taste of blood as he threw her to the ground. Red droplets landed on the pale carpet from her split lip, to the same rhythm as the rain pounding the ground outside. She let out a yell which was quickly followed by the sound of running feet.

"Wha've you done?" Tom screamed. "Who's comin'?"

Annabel said nothing, remaining crouched on the floor. Just as Tom reached out for her again a maid, in a thin nightgown and slippers, burst through the door. Seeing the foul man standing over her bleeding mistress she let out a loud, chilling scream and ran back down the corridor at break neck speed.

Tom laughed. "See, told ya we're alone."

However, within seconds a stampede of feet could be heard. It was Annabel's time to smile now as she saw Tom, from the corner of her eye, surveying the room for a hiding place. Before he had the chance to pick one at least ten male servants, all still in their pajamas, flew into the room. Without missing a beat a black haired, Italian looking man, grabbed hold of Tom's broad shoulders, throwing him to the ground. There was a pistol in his hand which he pointed square between Tom's eyes. Tom froze, genuine fear on his features for the first time, though he tried his hardest to hide it with another menacing grin.

Annabel rolled onto her back, her breathing heavy. The hot trickle of blood was still leaking from her lip, running down her chin and spreading across the neck of her nightgown.

"Miss Annabel!"

She heard her name called several times but seemed to be listening to the voices from a distance. She squeezed her eyes closed as tears leaked down from the corners of her eyes. Someone touched her shoulder and her eyes snapped open.

"We have sent for the police already Miss. Should I get a doctor?"

"No, please -"

"What on earth is all this ridiculous commotion?" She heard her father's voice boom through the halls before she had a chance to reply. "Does anyone in this house possess a watch? It is four in the bloody morning!"

The elder man rounded the corner into his daughter's bedchamber and froze, taking in the scene in front of him with wide eyes. Lord Hoddington simply stood in the doorway, his gaze flitting between his daughter, bleeding on the floor and Tom pinned at the other end of the room.

"Is this him? This is the brute you wish to marry over the most eligible bachelor in the country? I can't say I'm surprised that he's hit you Annabel." Looking now at Tom he said, "I do not know how you escaped prison but let me make this clear now, you will never see the light of day again, understand?"

"Father - no, it's not-"

"I've heard and seen enough Annabel. Be quiet." He looked around the room, glancing at the staff. "Are you all incompetent? Someone send for the police!"

"It's – it's already been done Sir," came a shy voice from the corner.

"Right, well-"

"Father, this is not Daniel!" Annabel shouted, unable to stay quiet anymore. "This is my captor. This man kidnapped me. Daniel helped me escape."

Her father took another step back from the room. He didn't like being proved wrong.

"Still," he said. "That's not the sort of family we are to be associated with. Daniel is staying where he is. This man will hang."

In reply Tom simply spat in the general direction of Annabel's father, laughing as the saliva landed on his velvet slippers.

It was an excruciating half an hour of near silence as they awaited the police. Annabel's father barked orders from a safe distance, as a maid tried to press a wet cloth to Annabel's face. Tom tried to fight, screaming out a string of profanities as he did so. He was overpowered every time.

Finally, the sound of hurried hooves filtered up from the drive, alerting everyone to the arrival of the police. Moments later Sergeant Link strode into the room, wielding a truncheon as if he were performing in a pantomime.

"That man, arrest him!" Annabel's father exclaimed, a look of disgust on his face. "And for God sake can someone get this damn room cleaned up, it looks a state!"

Annabel rose shakily to her feet as her father left the room. Approaching one of the officers she spoke in a whisper.

"This man is the one who kidnapped me, the one who took me on the thirtieth of May. The man you hold, Daniel Prince, he is innocent. Please believe me."

Tom screamed as he was placed roughly in handcuffs. He threw his weight around like a bull in a china shop, knocking over the officers in his attempt to break free. Some of Annabel's maids had now changed into their uniform and were clearing up around the struggle, studiously ignoring Tom. There was fear on all of their faces but they daren't disobey Lord Hoddington by ceasing their house work. One of them yawned and, catching Annabel's eye, quickly looked away as if ashamed.

"Here - I'll write it down," Annabel continued to plead with the officer, unfazed. She rifled through her bedside cabinet, pulling out a pen and small pad of embossed paper. She scribbled furiously until she had filled most of the pages in a matter of minutes. When she looked up the officers had gone. Fresh blood had now dried on her face, making the skin tight but she ignored her discomfort and ran down the hall.

"Officer!" she called desperately from the top of the stairs. Sergeant Link, who had been deep in conversation with Annabel's father, was the only one left. He turned around slowly, looking up at the young girl standing in a thin, blood splattered nightgown.

"Take this." Annabel shoved the paper into his hand. "I've signed it, it's my official statement. I will be prepared to testify in court if necessary. I know Daniel's not meant to have a trial but it's simply barbaric. Please see to it that he is released with all due haste."

The sergeant glanced at Lord Hoddington who gave him a pointed look. Link nodded and continued on his way. Annabel watched him leave. The spring in his step seemed strange. It was as if he had just received some good news. As if, perhaps, he had just made a particularly fortuitous deal. Annabel turned to her father.

"What have you done?" she whispered, her expression incredulous, whilst his was entirely passive. "WHAT HAVE YOU DONE?"

Chapter Twenty-One

As the dim sunlight, fighting against the grey rain clouds, pilfered through the window the next day, Annabel only vaguely recalled how her father's hand had struck her cheek. She had been shocked. Fury raged inside her like an inferno. Not long afterwards the same elderly doctor had bustled up the steps. No matter how hard she fought she was still too weak to throw off the doctor, her father and an army of butlers before the sedative was forced into her veins.

Coming back to the present Annabel shivered and finally swung her legs onto the carpet, imagining Billy, Patsy and Genevieve sleeping outside in this weather. Not thinking about the fact she was still in her nightclothes, her hair loose around her shoulders, she strode down the corridor, climbing down the east stairs and back up the west ones into her father's huge office. The office had two separate rooms to it, the first was a small sitting room housing two leather sofas, one on either side of a dark fireplace. Annabel pushed open a door to her left, finding her father seated behind an enormous, solid mahogany desk. The olive green walls were covered in books and files relating to various aspects of business Annabel had never inquired about. There were two leather armchairs on Annabel's side of the desk, matching the sofas in the sitting room. Her father was sat with raised eyebrows. He gestured for her to sit, leaning back in his own chair to give her his full attention. He crossed his hands over his rotund belly. His wedding ring shone as it caught the flickering light of his candle. There were no windows or electricity in this room of the house. Her father preferred to work in the dark, gloomy atmosphere.

"Have you quite recovered?" He looked her up and down as she sat there in her night clothes, her bare feet resting on the hard wood floor. She nodded although she could feel the throb of a bruise covering the lower portion of her face and knew her lip had swollen to twice its original size.

"Quite, I just took a slight turn is all. Being confronted with the man that kidnapped me Father, it was frightening. Anybody would have reacted the same way. He could have killed me, I hope you're aware of that. I was wondering though, about the friends I told you about."

He sighed in exasperation, not even acknowledging the information that she could have been murdered. He seemed under the impression the last few weeks had been a voluntary expedition for Annabel.

"If this is about that boy, we've already been over it Annabel. There is no chance of him being freed. I have paid off some officers and they have agreed to keep him comfortable. When his time is served he'll be given a job in the army. That's a respectable career for any man, especially one of his…background."

Annabel swallowed all of her foul retorts and tried to remember the current purpose of her visit.

"I wished to discuss Patsy and her brother Billy. They had a baby named Genevieve with them. I wanted to know what has become of them and I want them to have rooms in the manor."

"How did I create such an insufferable daughter? There is no way peasants can have rooms here unless they are employed-"

"Then see to it that they are." Annabel stood up. "Billy would work best with horses. Those people are the single reason I am alive Father, remember that when you are judging them so harshly."

He rubbed his hand over his eyes in a fake expression of exhaustion.

"I'll set some people on it at once but do get some rest Annabel, you look a fright."

"Summon me as soon as they are found and make sure it is prompt."

Lord Hoddington closed the door behind her with a little more force than was necessary when Annabel was ushered out only seconds later. She immediately made her way back to the east wing to bathe and dress. The maids laid out a white cotton gown with thin pink pinstripes. The fabric reached up to her neck and down to her wrists. Once she was dressed she made her way back downstairs and into her own writing room. In contrast to her mother and father's dingy domains this room was filled with pale furniture, fur rugs overlapping each other on the wooden floor. She sat behind her desk somewhat tentatively and composed a letter to the only person she could think of, Daniel. His face, as he was dragged away, trying to hold it together whilst he was clearly frightened and confused, filled her mind's eye constantly. Annabel knew there were no words to express all that had happened to them both in the last few weeks but after several attempts, she settled on this:

My dear Daniel,

I feel as if I have led you into a trap from which you cannot escape. I have been careless and selfish. For that, I must apologise from the very bottom of my soul.

I cannot even begin to fathom the idea of forming a life outside of you, especially when you are suffering so many unknown horrors. Have you not suffered enough? What kind of God would condemn such a beautiful man to this life?

I have sent Father to look for Billy and Patsy. I assure you I will find them as *soon as possible. The entire town will be looking for them if I have my way. I will let them stay here; to live with all the rich- es they could ever want — especially Gene- vieve, she'll be spoiled more than any child ever was. I will fight for you to be a part of our lives with every ounce of my own. I have tried to tell the police everything about Tom and Trevor, in the hope they will see you for the innocent man you are, but I fear the statement will deliberately go astray. Nothing I do now can right the wrongs I have done you but regardless I will keep trying. Until we next meet, which I hope to be soon, I give you my whole heart.*

Yours forever,

Anna

She slid the letter into an envelope, sealing it with a kiss before passing it to a servant with strict orders and a shiny penny she had stolen from her father's desk.

Her mother found her several hours later sitting in the now cold room. She walked over to the wall next to Anna- bel's desk, pulling a string that was attached to a wall of bells in the servant's quarters.

"Why are you sitting in here without a fire? You're supposed to be in bed and you need some lunch. What are you doing?"

"Thinking," she answered.

"About what child? Don't mumble, it's not becoming."

Annabel raised her head.

"About the innocent man who is being condemned to a lifetime of misery as we speak."

"Oh Annabel, please let it go."

"I can't let it go Mother, it's unjust."

"Since when did you care for such things?"

"Since I realised what a horrid person I was."

"You've never been a horrid person my dear, you have just known your position in society was higher than everyone else's."

"Do you hear yourself Mother? Why are you here anyway?"

Her mother sat down on one of the heavily stuffed arm chairs, her face flushed with pride.

"I have written to Lord Brogan with regards to your return and he is as excited as us for his son to see you. Theodore is a really perfect man Annabel, please try to like him. He will arrive in time for a late dinner in a week's time. Time enough for you to be looking at your best again." She sighed deeply, looking at Annabel's swollen face, which had crumpled into a dejected expression of misery, and placed her hand on her only child's.

"I do love you Annabel, please try to remember that."

She strode out of the door without offering any more reassurance, her posture as erect as always, unaware of the guilt she had instilled in her distraught daughter. Annabel felt as if she was being pulled in different directions by everybody, unable to please anyone without destroying the other.

Did she fight for the man she loved and destroy the lives of her family or destroy the other half of herself to please her blood and class? She wiped her eyes, accepting a tray the maid had brought into the room. As she nibbled absentmindedly on the plain food, taking the gulp of medicine left in a small crystal sherry glass, there was a knock on the door and Annabel looked up as the maid, now finished with the fire, opened it. Cuthbert, the head butler, walked in bowing.

"Miss," he greeted her.

"Cuddy," she smiled. He was a kind, jolly fellow that she had always been fond of. He smiled at this shortened version of his name, originating from an age when Cuthbert was too much of a mouthful.

"There are some visitors for you in the second parlour Madam."

"The second – did they leave a card? Who is it?" She shot to her feet.

"Well Miss they aren't...your father insisted you would want to-"

She grinned, joy spreading through her body. She sprinted past Cuddy and down the stairs, skidding to a stop just in front of the parlour door. She tore it open to reveal Patsy sat awkwardly in the chair closest to the door and Billy rocking Genevieve by the fire. She threw her arms around each of them in turn, squeezing so hard she feared she may break them.

"Can you bring us some tea please Cuddy?" she asked the butler who had followed her and was therefore now wheezing in the doorway. "And some plain ham sandwiches, you must be starved." She directed the last utterance towards her guests.

"Miss...aren't these people-"

"Do as I've asked please Cuddy, don't question me. These people are the reason I am alive and should be treated with reverence not disgust."

He bowed, backing out of the room. Annabel grinned at her friends.

"Oh and Cuddy, a bottle of milk for the baby as well, thank you."

"What happened to you?" Patsy broke the silence and Annabel's smile faded.

"The police found us, they assumed Daniel was my kidnapper and arrested him."

"No, we found tha' out ourselves. Wha' happened to your face?"

"I was visited by Tom last night."

Patsy gasped, clapping her hand to her mouth.

"It's alright, he has been arrested. He is locked up now, he shan't hurt you again Patsy. I can promise you that at least."

"Thank you," Patsy whispered. Her shoulders slumped

as if in relief and her eyes clouded over slightly.

"Please don't thank me. I've torn your family to shreds. Look at Daniel, locked away for crimes he never committed just because of his association to me. Which reminds me, you must adopt another surname, you cannot be Prince anymore, it's too dangerous."

"I don't want that name anyway," Patsy replied with her old fire.

Annabel sighed in relief at their cooperation.

"But, what about Daniel?"

"I don't know Patsy. I've tried everything I can think of. I've spoken to the police and to Father but I fear it will be no good. No-one will let me leave, they think my mind has gone. They are keeping me sedated. I couldn't leave even if I tried. But I miss him so much."

Billy came over and patted Annabel's head gently, she smiled up at him.

"You're pretty," he muttered. Annabel reached up and took his hand.

"Thank you Billy," her voice was thick. "You're very handsome yourself."

He puffed out his chest proudly and grinned, looking back down at Genevieve.

"Your papa says we can't stay in the house, he said if we 'ave to stay we'll sleep in the stable."

Annabel scoffed at Patsy's words.

"No you won't, you'll stay in my wing of the house. He simply can't object. I'll fill it with the best furniture I can find. I – I know it's not much but I can give you money if you want. If you don't want to stay I understand. I'll give you whatever you need."

The rest of her sentence was broken off as Patsy hugged her tightly.

"We don't want your things Anna, we jus' wanna see you."

"And you will, every day," she smiled. "Billy? Do you want to work with the horses? I told Father you're the best stable hand I ever saw. I don't want you to work for me, it seems so demeaning but Father...I don't know why he's being so difficult. I thought he'd understand."

The grin on Billy's face at the mention of horses was so large, she thought she might burst from the joy it caused in her breast.

"Billy work with rich horses?"

She nodded.

"An' live in the big house?"

She nodded again. "Jen will never go without anything."

She thought it impossible but Billy's smile grew even bigger, splitting his entire face in two. He was practically bouncing on the spot although Annabel felt she was giving them so little.

Just moments later, Cuthbert came back with a tray full of small sandwiches and a large pot of tea which Annabel made up for them. They ate greedily, Annabel watching them, happy she could at least give them some joy.

"Best food I've ever had," Patsy said, crumbs flying out of her mouth.

"You should taste the salmon," Annabel laughed, Patsy's forehead creased in confusion.

"Wha's salmon?"

"Oh um it's a fish. From – from the sea or river or something. It's really good, I'll bring you some soon but first you have to get used to less rich food. I made that mistake my first night back and was really ill so don't eat too much please."

They both stopped eating at the thought of getting sick. Instead they told Annabel all about how their horse had took off through the forest at some loud noise and they had found themselves in the main town. They had slept in an abandoned barn with holes in the roof for that first couple of nights, the weather being too bad to venture far. They had approached the big white house that very morning but been shooed away by the gatekeepers before they could even say their piece.

"Then a couple hours age some men in shiny clothes took us here."

"I told Father to look for you, I knew he would!"

"I don' think they like us much though."

"They don't like anyone much Patsy, trust me. They hate me with a passion. Follow me, I'll take you to my dressing room and get one of the maids to draw you up a bath."

Peeking out of the door, she ushered them out and up to her room where she rang the bell to get the fire lit, a bath drawn and two sets of clothes brought up. The maid looked shocked for a minute, glancing from Annabel to the two poor people and the baby sitting amongst the splendour of her quarters.

She returned with a simple black dress like the one the maids all wore, along with a pair of black trousers and a shirt for Billy. Bathing quickly, complimenting every one of Annabel's many possessions, they got changed behind the screen. Seeing them stood there in the household uniform Annabel was a little embarrassed at her own finery, glad she'd done up her hair simply and worn the cotton dress. She slid the fancy hair comb that Patsy had returned to her in the village, now polished back to its former glory, into Patsy's hair which the maid had arranged into a series of braids, twisted into a high bun with a few strands falling around her face to frame it perfectly.

"No Anna, I can't take that!"

"You found it, please take it."

"But it's yours."

Annabel laughed without humour.

"Patsy, I have a sickening amount of possessions, please take this one."

Patsy stared at herself in the mirror, even in the simple dress she looked awed at her reflection, gasping as Annabel draped a heavily embroidered shawl around her shoulders and fastened it with a solid gold brooch.

"There," she whispered. "I'm sorry it's not much but it's better than that thing." She glanced at the balled up brown dress Patsy had been wearing, just as the maid scooped it into her arms, holding it as far from her body as possible.

"Not much? Anna it's beautiful!" She twirled around, watching as her skirt ballooned around her ankles revealing the leather boots laced on her small feet.

"We'll have to visit my dress maker so you can get some dresses properly fitted."

Patsy practically shone with happiness.

"I wish Daniel could see this." Her face suddenly fell.

"Me too," Annabel whispered as a beautiful image of Daniel in tails flittered into her mind. She closed her eyes to stop the image fading but inevitably it did. She drew in a deep breath for courage and smiled at Patsy's reflection as Billy came back in, fiddling with the braces on his shoulders.

"You look handsome Billy," she said.

He stopped fidgeting and smiled.

"I know it's not as comfortable but you look really good."

He stood tall and proud, kissing her on the cheek and blushing at the compliment. He caught himself in the mirror and smiled wider, pointing at himself. They had fun bathing Genevieve next. She gurgled in happiness as the warm water soothed her tiny body, washing away the last traces of illness from her silken skin. With the right medicine and nutrition Annabel felt certain she'd be a healthy child. They fashioned undergarments for her and then wrapped her in a woollen shawl. Her pink face practically glowed. Annabel took a shawl for herself. Securing it around her shoulders, she led them back out of her room and down the labyrinth of corridors. Just before they reached the servant's quarters they found an empty corridor of rooms, less grand than the rest of the house but still expensive looking and somewhere her parents were unlikely to mind being used. They walked up to a door identical to all the others in the lengthy hall. Feeling for the cold door knob, Annabel swung it open.

"This will have to do for the moment, I'm sorry but I'll have fresh sheets brought in and we'll do it up as soon as possible."

The look of joy that crossed over the two faces standing before her, just at the sight of a guest suite, broke Annabel's fragile heart, making her realise how ridiculously over the top the rest of the house was. The suite had a small living room containing one large, cosy looking sofa, set before a tiled fireplace. Three doors led off of it into an adjoining bedroom, dressing room and another much smaller room of no apparent purpose.

"I'll have some proper furniture put in tomorrow and some more food brought up soon." She whispered. "I'll come and see you as often as I can. Please don't leave. I feel sick offering you this after you saw my room."

"Don't Anna. It's the best home we've ever had."

"But it's still not enough," she glanced up at them. "You deserve all the riches in the world."

She kissed each of their foreheads carefully and walked over to the sofa. Patsy took a seat beside her and clasped Annabel's hand in her own. It was hot and clammy.

"Thank you."

Annabel closed her eyes and squeezed back Patsy's

hand.

"You all mean the world to me, truly."

None of them heard the door open at first, nor the soft footfalls of the doctor, until he was stood in front of the sofa.

"Miss Annabel, you were instructed to stay in bed."

Chapter Twenty-Two

The rest of the week passed in a sedated blur with Annabel believed too mentally unstable to be awake for longer than it took to eat. On the Saturday morning, when Annabel had awoken to a strange, unfamiliar sense of clarity, only to be confronted by two butlers clearly working as her prison guards, Annabel found her mother seated at the foot of her bed.

"Why are you here?" Annabel demanded, shifting so she was out of the woman's reach.

Her mother simply looked up at the ceiling in exasperation.

"Today you are to meet Theodore, remember? Put your ring on. The engagement is to be announced in the paper today. A much less lavish announcement than I had planned but the first ball was ruined."

"No! But-"

"There are no buts Annabel, you are going to marry him and now the entire world knows it."

"Then you are going to be sorely disappointed Mother for I shall not. Not after the way you have treated all the people who had a hand at saving my life!"

"They only needed to do, whatever it was they did, because you wondered off in the first place Annabel."

Annabel chose to ignore that statement. So someone had seen her leave the park after all. "Where are Billy and Patsy? What have you done with them?"

"The peasant and the idiot?" her mother scoffed.

Annabel leapt up with a surprising amount of agility and seized the woman's shoulders in a vice like grip. Her mother looked on, startled.

"Don't EVER call them that again! Those people have more courage, more intelligence and more love than anyone I have ever met. How dare you degrade them with such titles?"

"Get off me Annabel. They are working in the house. The male is our new stable hand, the girl in the kitchen. They are still staying in the rooms you put them in, in direct disobedience of your father's orders I may add. And whilst you're telling me how to behave in my own house, I don't want to see you fraternising with the staff, you understand? I catch you with them just once and they will no longer be able to call this their home. Don't forget, we could always extend Daniel's sentence. I don't think he would think too kindly of you if he had to stay in prison forever now would he?"

Annabel let go of her mother quickly, disgusted by the mere sight of her. The elder woman stood up, smoothing down her skirts as if the conversation that had passed between them was one of the utmost civility.

"Theodore Brogan shall be here for an early dinner this

evening. I'll send some maids in so you look somewhat like your old self." The woman sighed. "One half of me wishes you had not been found, you have changed so unrecognisably."

That stung Annabel more than anything else and she sat back down on her crumpled bed covers, lacking the energy or will to even move.

The maids came in, as expected, as soon as Lady Hoddington left the room to prepare their mistress to meet the man everyone wanted her to marry, whilst she couldn't remove the image of the one man she wanted.

For the dinner that night she chose a dress as close to mourning colour as she could get away with. It was a deep silvery grey, embellished with white ostrich feathers at the hem which flowed into a sweeping train. The sleeves puffed out at the shoulders and fit snug just above her elbows, where they were met with long white opera gloves. In her ears hung a pair of diamond and sapphire earrings, a matching necklace rested just above her chest. She looked simply perfect; no one who caught sight of her could deny that fact. Slipping her feet into a pair of beaded, high heeled slippers she tried to swallow the huge swell of grief, guilt and betrayal that threatened to swamp her. Taking a deep breath and composing her face into a hard, emotionless mask, she made her way down the stairs; placing herself to catch the light just perfectly in such a vain manner it had her clutching her stomach in a sudden burst of nausea.

Once in sight of the most elaborate of the parlours, her

mother rose to her feet, dressed in a fitted red velvet gown that complimented her dark hair, swept up in a more carefully constructed version of her usual tight bun. Her throat, ears, wrists and hair shone with diamonds every time she moved.

Lord Hoddington stood by the large fire that could be a room in itself, wearing an expensively tailored suit and tails in a deep black, a red cravat secured with a diamond pin at his throat to match his wife. This parlour had an ornately painted, high ceiling dripping with crystal chandeliers fit for royalty. The carvings on the fireplace depicted angels and cherubs to match the ceiling. Every piece of the expensive furniture had been specifically placed to show off the family's wealth to the best possible advantage. There were paintings done by the most famous artists in the world covering almost every inch of the walls. Three floor to ceiling windows across the left hand wall overlooked both the drive and the best section of the grounds. A portrait of the three current Hoddingon's hung above the fire, reflecting them in all their splendour. A large set of double doors off to the right led to the main dining room dressed with equal splendour.

"Well done Annabel, you look almost perfect," her mother said approaching her. "Although you could have chosen a brighter colour."

Annabel gave her no recognition and simply walked past her to sit in a high backed chair by the window.

"No, sit here," her mother gestured to a chair closer to the door. "That way you'll be the first thing he sees."

She did as she was told, obediently waiting for Theodore to arrive in silence, her hands folded demurely in her lap whilst her mind wandered to the night spent with Daniel touching every inch of her skin. Slightly flushed she stood as Cuthbert came in to the room. Reflexively she smoothed her skirt so it fell down her legs in a perfect sweep of silk, the feathers swaying slightly.

"Mister Theodore Brogan," Cuddy announced, bowing as Theodore came into view.

He was a few inches taller than Daniel, probably just over six feet, his cheekbones and jaw sharp, as if carved from marble. His hair, combed back off his face, was a rich, chocolate brown whilst his bright eyes matched the shade exactly. He was perfectly handsome in every way, as if made from textbook instructions. His smile revealed a set of straight, pearly white teeth as he strode confidently up to her, placing Annabel's gloved hand to his lips. She dipped into a curtsey.

"A pleasure to meet you, Sir."

"Likewise Miss, you are simply radiant."

She smiled but it did not touch her eyes.

"I hope you are well following your ordeal." His voice was as smooth as silk, educated to the highest degree.

"I am flattered by your concern Sir yet you find me quite recovered."

"Please Miss Hoddington, do call me Teddy."

He smiled at her again and she noticed how good that smile would have made her feel just a few weeks ago. It illuminated his entire face, making his dark eyes sparkle, yet she couldn't help comparing him to Daniel.

Teddy's fingers were thinner, making them look almost feminine. His face was so flawless in comparison to Daniel's freckled, scarred features that she knew he had seen little of the real world outside of fancy ballrooms and manor houses. Moving to the side, still smiling, he approached her mother, kissing her hand as well.

"Always lovely to see you Lady Hoddington."

She flushed slightly, still affected by his beauty despite him being half her age. Her father clapped him on the back.

"Grayson," Teddy greeted, shaking his hand. "A pleasure."

"Was your journey pleasant Mister Brogan?"

"Quite as pleasant as can be expected Lord Hoddington, yes."

Teddy kept his hands clasped behind his back, his spine as straight as a board. Annabel watched him converse with her parents. Even the slightest movements of his face were exactly as they should have been. His dark eyebrows raised themselves only a fraction when Annabel's mother reluctantly began telling her daughter's tale.

"Oh, do not fuss Mister Brogan. It has all been rather exaggerated in the papers as I am sure you can understand."

Teddy glanced across at Annabel, his mouth opening ever so slightly as if to ask the younger woman a question, however Annabel's mother continued.

"Indeed Annabel was taken from the park on the day

of her birthday, by men who wished to acquire her fortunes."

"I am sorry to hear that Miss-"

"Don't be sorry dear boy, my daughter is very well. She was not gone from us long and certainly wasn't mistreated in any way."

Theodore nodded, giving Annabel a small smile. She saw a flicker of kindness in his chocolate eyes just as a butler emerged to announce dinner. Teddy offered his arm which Annabel took, although she tried to avoid touching him as much as possible. Annabel was helped into her chair, just as Teddy's tutor had no doubt taught him. Her heart hurt, it would have been so much easier to disappoint him if he was horrible. He deserved so much more than her. She felt as if she were already married, she was in every way beside the law. This evening felt like adultery, betrayal of the highest order. Teddy could not have been more perfect if she had designed him herself but he wasn't Daniel.

Following dinner they made their way back to the parlour to be served champagne for the women and brandy for the gentlemen, making some more idle chit chat that seemed incredibly pointless to Annabel. Once darkness had descended Annabel's father stood up.

"Theodore, we must retire to the smoking room and leave the women to their sewing." He laughed and Teddy stood up.

"You're right Sir. Miss Annabel is looking slightly fatigued and is quite within reason to be after her ordeal."

He smiled at her, his eyes glittering. Annabel stood as he bent to kiss her hand again. "Until next we meet, it has been an honour."

He kissed her mother as well and followed Lord Hoddington into the smoking room, no doubt to discuss Annabel and other successful business ventures. Annabel followed them as far as the east stairs; she could feel her mother glaring at her the entire way.

Once back in the sanctuary of her room she dismissed her maids and finally surrendered to the racking sobs that had been threatening to spill over all evening, clutching Daniel's carving to her chest.

At some point during the night Annabel felt the sharp pain of the sedative being reintroduced to her blood stream and her mind fogged over once more. She realised at that moment that, in her half-conscious state of mind, she had been calling out to Daniel. The sheets were drenched in cold sweat and tangled around her thrashing limbs.

When she came to, the elderly doctor was seated beside her. A thermometer had been pushed into her mouth and he was frowning.

"Ah Miss Annabel, you're awake. How are you feeling today?"

"Like death warmed up Doctor. Why do you insist on sedating me? What do you think it will do?"

"It is by your mother's request my dear and you do seem to be quite over excited of late. Rest will do you some good. But now please answer me. Are there any symptoms you may be feeling that would hint to a diagnosis for you? Are you nauseas at all?"

At that moment Annabel did in fact feel very sick but she bit it back and shook her head.

"Any aches and pains?"

Again she shook her head.

The doctor gave her a look, telling her he wasn't fooled and noted down her temperature.

"Do you know what happened to Daniel? That is the cause of my upset Doctor, to know that he is-"

"Stop worrying Miss. The man has been sentenced to ten years. It was in the papers this morning. Bludgeoned his own father to death, makes you think doesn't it? There was something about the police going to rescue two small boys, the father was found dead in his own bed."

"What? No!"

"Yes, his own brother gave evidence for the crime. Although I must say he fared even worse, apparently he has been abusive for years. Five charges of murder were swinging over his head if you excuse the pun. He is to be hung tomorrow I think. It's all happened very quickly, usually these kinds of trials take months or even years. Someone very powerful must want them out of the way is all I can think of. Are you sure you're quite alright Miss? You've gone rather pale."

Annabel was breathing heavily, her eyes wide. Ten years. So it was official...but then, would ten years be that long to wait? She would be twenty eight...that was still young enough."

The door opened slowly, startling her from her reverie.

"Annabel, good to see you awake finally."

"Get to the point Mother."

The older woman sighed.

"No fooling you is there? Never was. Mister Brogan is waiting to receive you in the main parlour."

"What? I thought he left."

"No, he is staying here until we can decide on a date for the wedding."

"Well he'll be waiting a while."

Looking angry, her mother summoned a maid to fix Annabel's hair so it was pinned in an elegant design and laced her into a pale blue day dress.

"There, that looks better," her mother declared, pinching her daughter's cheeks when she was finally deemed presentable. "Now go, you've kept him waiting long enough and for goodness sake try not to look like you're walking to your execution."

"But I am," Annabel muttered under her breath.

When she entered the parlour Theodore was stood by the fire, wearing a light brown suit, his hat twitching against his knee. He jumped when he caught her looking at him, quickly rearranging his features into a smile.

"Miss Annabel, you're looking as lovely as ever."

"How would you know Mister Brogan? This is the second time you've ever met me."

He laughed, unsure whether she was joking or not. To alleviate the awkwardness Annabel gestured to a pair of arm chairs by the window.

"Take a seat," she muttered.

A small table was placed between them, housing tea and small cakes. Unthinking, Annabel picked one up, immediately stuffing it into her mouth. Teddy pretended not to see, suppressing a smile behind his elegant hand.

"How do you take your tea?" he asked, looking up. "It seems absurd that I can know so much about you but not how you take your tea." He was stiff and formal, afraid of saying the wrong thing.

"Sugar and lemon please, no cream."

"I wanted to speak with you alone. I thought, given the circumstances, we shouldn't need chaperones."

Annabel smiled, stirring her tea absentmindedly. The silver spoon clinked against the china as she did so, the noise sounded loud in the awkward atmosphere.

"What are the circumstances Mister Brogan?"

"Well, that we are, if you are still agreeable to the idea of course, going to marry."

Annabel sipped her tea, desperate to change the topic. Theodore continued in a low whisper, his voice hesitant.

"What really happened to you?"

Annabel was somewhat surprised by his forwardness.

"I've already told you Mister Brogan," she smiled with what she hoped was kindness.

"Teddy please, Mister Brogan is my father's name. With respect, I believe your mother altered your tale considerably through fear I would run away. I don't believe anything that happened to you can have been your fault Miss, for the record."

"Why do you insist that I call you Teddy if you cannot call me Annabel? Given the circumstances, don't you think that might be necessary?"

"Of course...Annabel," he sipped his tea, looking thoughtfully out the window.

"It's a lovely house you have here, beautiful. The house I spend most of my time in is very dingy. Father likes dark colours, hardly any light in the whole place. What with Mother having passed some years ago, there isn't a hint of femininity there at all."

They sat for the next ten minutes sipping on their tea, neither one knowing the appropriate thing to break the heavy silence. Finishing her cup Annabel excused herself, retiring to her bedchamber on the pretense of dressing for dinner. She did not believe for one minute staying had been Theodore's idea but more her mother's way of ensuring her daughter would marry him.

Her bath was drawn up and she lay in the warm water until her fingertips grew wrinkled. She found that when her head was submerged every noise was muffled, as if coming from behind a wall, giving off the illusion she had entered a different world entirely. Her maids dismissed for an hour she ran her fingers lightly over her flawless skin, remembering when it had been longer, rougher fingers doing this. She longed for Daniel's touch so much it physically hurt, wondering why he had not even replied to her letter.

Coming back up to the surface, her lungs burning for air, she dried herself off and rang the bell, getting laced into yet another silk gown. This one was a lighter silver than the one she was wearing the day before, with golden lace sleeves which sparkled when caught by the light. The neckline was scooped, showing a small amount of her snow white flesh which she adorned with a jewelled necklace, her hair swept into an array of pinned up curls and glittering hair combs.

Over the next few days her mother talked of nothing but Theodore, going on about how stunning a couple he and her daughter would be out in high society, flushed with so much pride Annabel couldn't bare it. Daniel was now in Annabel's every waking thought. She felt as if she wasn't doing enough for him yet was at a loss what more could be done. Whenever the topic was approached she was shot down. Her parents had now taken to inviting Theodore to all of their meals as they knew she would not dare discuss Daniel around him - although, she was on the brink of it. It was only her mother's threat that Daniel's sentence could be extended holding her tongue.

Annabel was told the decorating of Billy and Patsy's quarters had been started and ended just two days later. The furniture had been taken from empty rooms in the east wing of the house to make the job quicker. The cosy sitting room still had the highly stuffed sofa in front the fire but now also housed two plump arm chairs on either side of it and an elaborately woven rug. The smallest room was made into Genevieve's room with a single sleigh bed and a wooden dolls house, surrounded by all of Annabel's old dolls sat on a set of shelves along the wall. A new teddy bear lounged on the pink lace covers, a writing desk in the corner. Billy's room (fashioned from what was a dressing room) housed a four poster bed now draped with a large canopy of midnight blue silk, embroidered with tiny silver stars. Genevieve's temporary crib sat in the corner. Patsy's room was the biggest of the three bedrooms with a queen sized bed covered in bronze coloured, satin covers. A large mahogany wardrobe stood at the end of the bed, a small fireplace on the right hand wall. Despite the rich furnishings, the best thing about the small apartment was the happiness and love that seemed to fill all of the rooms, making them instantly appear warm and safe.

The staff had grown to love the three new comers almost as much as Annabel, now not even questioning it when they saw their mistress huddled on the rug by the fire, even though she was supposed to be sedated in bed. None of the staff had the heart to tell the Lord and Lady Hoddington where their daughter really was.

Chapter Twenty-Three

After three long weeks with still no definite wedding date, Theodore took his leave from Hoddington manor to attend to business up country. He and Annabel had continued to speak only at meal times with one small turn around the garden where he tried to discuss their upcoming nuptials without success. His goodbye was as polite as should be expected from any noble gentleman, with the promise he would write as soon as he was able. Annabel could have loved him, in her old life before Daniel, but now she must hurt him, or go through life never being a true wife...the wife he deserved. She found it unfair that someone who had once not even wanted to fall in love could be thrown into the path of two perfect men, each vying for her heart.

She made her way slowly back up to her room, nausea rising up her throat with the movement of her steps. By the time Annabel reached her bedchamber she was very close to passing out, her breathing was coming so fast. The nausea she had felt earlier rose with vengeance into her throat causing her to bend over her chamber pot and empty her breakfast into it. Once she had, she fell back onto her heels, holding her head.

"Miss Hoddington, are you alright?" asked a maid, lingering at the door.

"Yes, everything is fine. Can you bring a glass of water and some medicine please? I am feeling quite faint all of a sudden."

The maid curtseyed and left with a short, "yes Miss."

She spent the rest of the day in a daze. She brushed her teeth and took her medicine however the nausea passed as quickly as it had come about. She sat on her bed for a long while, tracing the detailed carving of Daniel's face absentmindedly.

Lunch was brought up to her on a tray, the nausea creeping back in when Annabel smelt the sauce from the silver gravy boat. She ate a piece of bread and ordered the tray to be removed at once. The maid gave her a concerned glance but Annabel just lay down on top of her covers and faced the wall.

The doctor was summoned for, as Annabel knew he would be and he asked her the same questions as before. She told him that yes, she had felt sick but that it was just stress, she was sure of it. She tried desperately to get him to leave but he refused.

"I must get to the bottom of this illness Miss Annabel. It is quite peculiar that you should be suffering for such a long time after your ordeal has ended."

"But my ordeal is not over Doctor. An innocent man has been condemned and it is my fault."

Tears bloomed in her eyes and cascaded down her

cheeks.

"Now hush hush Miss, none of that can have been your fault. The two men that were condemned were villains, criminals of the highest order. Only ten years for bludgeoning your own father-"

"It was me."

"Sorry?"

"I bludgeoned his father. He was going to attack me, would you have preferred that?"

The doctor looked on with wide eyes, his mouth agape.

"What has gotten into you? Do not repeat such foul statements outside of this room!"

"Why does no-one wish to accept the truth? I am not the perfect girl that I once was. I was never that person, I have woken up now doctor and I can see the world for the harsh place it really is."

"You are clearly far worse than I had originally diagnosed. Please lie down."

"I am not crazy!"

"I never said you were. Such a diagnosis would ruin me even if it were true. You need to rest."

"Just tell me what is wrong doctor and then leave. I just want to know the facts."

Annabel listed the symptoms she had been feeling. The doctor asked her several follow up questions of the most untoward nature before placing his hands on her lower abdomen.

"What are you doing?" Annabel flinched at the touch.

"It is quite peculiar," he muttered.

"What is? Tell me doctor?"

"Well, the signs all point to one conclusion Miss Annabel but I can't see how it is possible. It appears - excuse me for saying it - that you are with child."

Annabel sat up sharply, her head spinning. Surely she had heard wrong?

"Wh-what did you say?"

"You are carrying a baby."

"But - that is quite impossible."

The doctor smiled sympathetically.

"It appears not."

It was a sin to have a child out of wedlock. Her family would never speak to her again. The entire world would disown her...the child would be shunned. Yet, throughout all of that, she felt a kind of warmth flooding through her. She tried to picture what Daniel had looked like as a child. With his white blonde hair and large hazel eyes, he would have been picture perfect. She put her hand against her stomach, unable to feel anything. It can't have been there more than five weeks but the knowledge she was carrying even the smallest part of Daniel, filled her with a joy she thought she'd never feel again and she grinned.

"Excuse my impertinence Miss but is the child indeed Mister Brogan's?"

Making up her mind in a matter of seconds, wrenching her thoughts away from a tiny baby with Daniel's hazel eyes, she answered.

"Of course - of course it is Theodore's child. Do you think a man spends three weeks under the same roof as his future wife and expects nothing in the way of...that."

"Well I - of course not, I just -"

The doctor looked at her doubtfully. He knew three weeks were not enough time to be showing the signs of pregnancy but once more, to suggest such a scandal would be his ruin.

"You just took me for a whore. I will tell Theodore myself after our wedding Doctor and if this information is released you will face such a ruin you will never be able to work again."

The doctor stood up, placing his equipment back inside his bag.

"Then I wash my hands of you. I will tell your parents you are quite healed but you need another day's bed rest. I trust you will protect my diagnosis by acting well?"

"Yes - yes of course. Thank you Doctor."

"If I'd considered the deceit this job would entail I would have skipped the middle man and gone straight into politics. Good day to you Miss Annabel, do not call on me again."

The doctor did not wait for a returned greeting. He simply tipped his hat slightly and rushed out of the door, his leather bag swinging at his side.

That night Annabel picked at her dinner, eating it on a silver tray in her room just as the doctor had ordered. The smell of the meat and gravy turned her stomach although Annabel smiled, knowing what that implied. When she had finished she slipped a shawl around her shoulders and crept down to Patsy and Billy's rooms, where she would spend the night with the only people who would understand how she felt.

When she told them about the child they both jumped with joy, wrapping her into such a tight embrace she couldn't breathe.

"Oh Daniel will be so pleased! He'll make a great Papa." Patsy exclaimed without thinking.

Annabel grinned, hugging her again.

"Oh he will be perfect won't he?"

Patsy's face suddenly fell.

"But he's - he's in jail Anna."

Annabel's eyes glazed over as her throat tightened.

"He can't know."

"What? But you jus' said -"

Annabel took her arm, leading Patsy into her room so the two girls could talk in private.

"He cannot know whilst he's in prison, it would drive him mad."

Patsy looked as though she wanted to argue but seemed to see the truth in these words.

"What's gunna happen to 'im?" Patsy whispered.

Annabel hesitated for a long while but knew she would have to tell her eventually.

"He - he has been sentenced to ten years. Tom has been hung."

"No. Daniel - but he's innocent."

"They charged him with the attack on Trevor. I tried to say it was me, I wrote a statement but I fear my father has gotten rid of it somehow. He felt threatened. He told me he paid the police to keep him in jail. I'm so sorry Patsy. This is my fault entirely."

"It ain't your fault Anna. It weren't you that put 'im in jail. It were your folks. And anyway, prison's still gotta be better than the village. If it weren't for you we'd still be there."

"Please Patsy." The understanding in Patsy's face was driving Annabel mad. She wanted her to be angry, to lash out at her. But she simply took her hand.

"We're strong Anna. We'll be okay." She looked up, fire in her eyes, "you'll 'ave to marry Theodore."

"Not you too Patsy. Please, I can take it from everyone else but not you."

Patsy did get angry now, she dropped Annabel's hand, frowning.

"So you'll leave behind all o' this?"

She waved her hands to indicate the luxuries of the manor. "The money an' the power, so tha' your baby can be a bastard? So tha' it will be an outcast? No Anna."

Annabel let out a strangled sob and Patsy folded her into her embrace, patting her back maternally.

"It's a hard world Anna. We gotta make the best of what we got."

When Annabel had dried her tears she lay down on Patsy's bed, suddenly too tired to even move a single muscle. She woke up curled on top of Patsy's blanket due to the heat of the sticky summer's night. In the end, she had only managed an hour or two of restless sleep, her mind whirring all night. She sat up slowly, her muscles heavy and sore. As she rose to her feet nausea once more swept over her. Placing a hand on her stomach she took several deep breaths before making her way back to her own bed chambers.

Her mother found her later that morning huddled in the middle of her bed, the sheets pulled up over her head, despite the heat. The wooden carving was once more pressed into her hand. Lady Elizabeth sat down, pulling the covers off of Annabel's slight frame, drawing in a breath at the state of her raw eyes and matted hair.

"Annabel."

Annabel said nothing, choosing just to lie back against her pillows.

"I'm sick Mother, please let me sleep."

"You're not sick you're wallowing. I'm sick of seeing you like this. I am sending in a maid, you're going to bathe, eat and come downstairs immediately. The doctor said you were fine. Your engagement ball is this weekend, you have a dress fitting to attend and then we are going for lunch. It will do you good to be out in society again."

Annabel dressed carefully, summoning for Patsy - much to her mother's distain - who helped her with her corset, leaving it a tiny bit looser than she would have usually worn it. She put on a pale pink summer dress, which was heavily embroidered and beaded with exquisite pearls. Both girls ate their breakfast sitting back on Annabel's bed, holding the knowledge that she was feeding more than just herself and now had to be especially careful when it came to missing meals. Once finished she took Patsy's arm and walked her down to her own room, where she dressed in a similar, yet less elaborate, suit of a warm beige. The colour complimented her hair, which had turned a slightly more fiery shade with the expensive soaps. The two girls were beginning to feel a sense of hope when they met Lady Elizabeth out on the drive, by the very same golden carriage Annabel had used all those weeks before on her eighteenth birthday.

"Who is this?" Lady Elizabeth asked, looking at Patsy with distrust.

"Patricia Pierce. She is my distant cousin, on father's side of course. She has come to stay with us for a while."

"This is the-"

"The cousin? Yes."

"Annabel you will ruin us all bringing people like that out in society."

"Mother, you will ruin my patience if you protest."

"Get in the carriage. Come on, hurry up!"

Lady Elizabeth conversed little with Patsy, choosing instead to look her up and down in a silent judgement. It seemed she could find nothing amiss with the young woman; Patsy was dressed as properly as if she had lived in the higher classes since birth and her hands, in an imitation of Annabel, were folded in her lap, exactly as they should be.

Annabel had spent many an hour already with Patsy working on her diction so she even sounded more like a high society girl. She was proving to be incredibly intelligent, picking up manners and information with an almost photographic memory. She even managed to contain her facial expression at the sight of the carriage, standing ornately in the driveway, although she did let out a slow wink towards Billy when she noticed him leading a horse towards the stables.

Their first stop was the dress makers. Its high, perfectly arranged windows gleamed even in the over cast, muggy weather. The second they stepped inside they were ushered into a private suite, arranged with cream and pale pink furnishings, filled with the most expensive of the shop's items. They were seated and handed tea in fancy bone china cups before being presented with roll after roll of fabric for them to choose from. Annabel gasped at an emerald green shade.

"Patsy that would look just divine on you, it would suit you so well!"

The sales girl smiled, placing the roll amongst the others that had been short listed.

"Well I don't see why you're picking a shade for her Annabel. You can't expect her to come to the ball."

"Mother, Patsy is my cousin if you remember. You can't very well expect her to miss it now, can you? Besides, the young girl of which we speak is in fact in the room, if you wish to discuss her, you could have the manners to direct the conversation to her personally."

Her mother pursed her lips, shaking her head at another roll of fabric but said nothing else on the matter. A couple of hours later they had each chosen the material for their dresses along with several materials for other less important dresses and accessories, to be charged to the family account. They were now sat in a warm restaurant filled with society's elite women and the odd few journalists, who began scribbling furiously the second they walked in. This was, after all, Annabel's first outing in society since she had gone missing.

The room smelt of expensive perfume and sugar, the tinkling sounds of chatter filled the air. Patsy looked awed by the place, its large windows, the golden chandeliers dripping from the ceiling in large upside down triangles, the pink silk walls and the elaborate displays of fresh roses on each table, seemed to have knocked all the air out of her. Even the food looked like a work of art, the cakes all iced with fancy designs, the plates arranged just so. The taste was exquisite as well although, of course, it would seem improper to gorge oneself on food in public so the three of them sat with straight backs, sipping tea and taking tiny bites from the ornate plates in front of them. Annabel found it thrilling to have Patsy with her, to know she was breaking her mother's rules right in front of her. To get the chance to view her world through Patsy's fresh, innocent eyes put everything in sharp perspective.

A lot of people came up to speak to them whilst they ate, all wanting to hear firsthand about the story they had read in the papers. To all of them Annabel held the same air of impatient distance that she was famed for. When she had to, she told them all the same thing; she was "quite recovered but rehashing the old tale is not in my interests. I simply want to move forwards. Oh, have you met my cousin Patricia Pierce? She has come to live with us for a while."

Thus, the conversation moved onto the fabricated past Annabel and Patsy had made up. They had decided on the surname Pierce as it was still similar to her original name and would therefore lead to the least confusion.

Her mother wittered on about the ball and the engagement, glancing to the side every time she did to reassure herself that Annabel wouldn't argue the point in public.

Annabel had desperately tried to avoid thinking about all that the ball implied. She had the entire future of both her and her unborn child's life to decide and under a week to do it in.

By the end of the day they had planned pretty much every aspect of the ball, from parchment for the invitations, to the exact colour of the corset she would wear under her dress. It was a welcome distraction. However, when she returned home the thoughts came thick and fast. She excused herself to her writing room where she composed a list of her options. She thought about how she would go about getting rid of the child, where she could go to have the child whilst she waited the ten years for Daniel but the option that made the most sense had her stomach turning violently, her eyes clouding over. It was the option Patsy had already told her. She knew this option was the only way it could work. This was the option that would be best for her child, the selfless option. Picking up her pen, she wrote a letter to Theodore.

Rebecca M. Gibson

Teddy,

I am sure you have already been invited in a much more formal way than this however, as your future wife, I wished to invite you myself to Hoddington Manor this week-end for the celebration of our engagement. I should very much like to marry you as soon as possible. I feel we have both waited long enough already.

I do hope this letter finds you well,

Annabel Hoddington

Folding the letter in two she leant back in the chair, feeling as if she had just signed away her life.

In something of a frenzy, Annabel raced downstairs, almost colliding with her mother at the foot of them. Annabel threw the crisp letter at her mother's feet.

"Read it!" she demanded.

The older woman picked it up gingerly, a small smile playing on her lips as she read her daughter's calligraphy.

"Annabel, my child, I knew you would come to your senses."

"Can you at least let me say goodbye," Annabel whispered.

"Goodbye to whom for heaven's sake?"

"To Daniel Mother, please."

"Whatever can you want to see that man for?"

"Just let me say goodbye Mother and I promise, I will do everything you ask. I will marry Theodore, I will provide you with all the heirs you want. I will be your perfect daughter again Mother. You just have to let me see him, one final time."

"I shan't allow it. You cannot bargain with me Annabel. You will marry Theodore whether your conditions have been met or not."

"See, you don't get it do you Mother? I don't care about your riches or your promises. You can put me in a white dress, you can drag me down the aisle but in the end, it's me that has to say I do and if you don't let me see Daniel, or if you threaten me or my new cousins, I will tell the entire church about my illicit love affair in the forest and you will be ruined. That's the thing about having nothing to lose, you have everything to gain."

Lady Elizabeth took a step back, dumbfounded.

"You wouldn't dare. Your reputation-"

"The reputation already built on lies? I don't care about it Mother. That is the difference between you and me. Let me see Daniel now, or watch your life crumble into dust."

Her mother stood stock still for several minutes, her mouth moving as if to form words but always remaining silent.

"You are to take a cab, not one of the manor's carriages," she blurted out eventually. "Wear something dark and inconspicuous. You mustn't be seen Annabel. You have one hour."

Annabel raced upstairs without missing a beat, fleeing straight into the servant's quarters.

"Does anyone have a cloak?" she called when she reached the kitchen.

The staff all turned around, their foreheads creased in worry.

"Please, can I borrow a cloak from someone, I need to go into town and I don't want to be mobbed whilst I am there. Please."

One girl, looking about fourteen in age, stepped towards her warily, wiping her floury hands on her apron.

"I - I have one miss."

An elderly woman beside her gave her a look but the girl continued to advance.

"Thank you," Annabel held out a shiny penny which the girl grabbed, beaming before running off, coming back with a thick, dark grey cloak of a scratchy material.

"I shall return it in an hour. Do you know where Patsy is? Patricia Pierce."

"Erm - I think she was visiting Billy in the stable. I can go fetch her if you like Miss?"

"If you would, thank you."

The girl rushed away again, returning once more within a matter of moments, a smiling Patsy trailing behind her.

"Anna, what's happened?"

Patsy looked at her with concern, noticing the frazzled

look on Annabel's face, the wildness in her eyes.

"We're going to see Daniel. I've got to say goodbye Patsy, I can't stand to just leave him."

Patsy seized Annabel's arm, dragging her out of the kitchen and into the stairwell where they could be alone.

"You can't tell him!"

"I wasn't - I know what's at stake here Patsy."

"I know you do Anna, I was jus' checking."

"And I love you for it."

Patsy smiled as Annabel gave her a kiss on the cheek and then took her hand, leading her out of the back door and down to the servants gate, after securing her own dark cloak so she too would be unrecognisable, their hoods pulled down over their eyes.

They flagged down a cab at the foot of the hill, both panting from the speed they had walked to get there. Annabel flashed a handful of shiny coins and the driver grinned, taking them to the station at lightning speed.

When they reached the entrance Annabel glanced at Patsy, who looked as if she might be sick.

"He will be alright won't he?" Annabel asked.

Patsy nodded, "eventually."

She squeezed Annabel's hand in her own; it was warm and sweaty with nerves.

"You're doing the right thing Anna."

Annabel nodded again and they climbed out of the cab, creeping up the steps and through to the dark entrance. There was a desk directly in front of them with a uniformed officer sat behind it. Annabel lowered her hood.

"Ah, Miss - Miss Hoddington. Your mother sent a telegram. It arrived just two minutes ago."

He looked uncertainly at Patsy, "and what are you here for?" he asked in a manner that could have been far more polite.

"This is my cousin Patricia, she is here for the same purpose I am. She wishes to extend her thanks to my tragically imprisoned saviour."

The officer looked as if he were going to protest but seemed to think better of it, realising with whom he was in fact speaking. Annabel placed a shiny guinea on the desk and he slid it into his palm.

"For your discretion," Annabel added.

"Of course Miss, please follow me." He took up a large bunch of keys and strapped them to his belt before escorting them through a narrow door off to the left of the desk.

They walked down the corridor, swathed in an eerie darkness, with what Annabel believed to be deliberate slowness. Several gates were unlocked and clanged shut behind them before finally they reached another corridor, lined with cells. The cells all seemed to be empty, the corridor was deadly silent. One cell had its door wide open with what looked like an office set up inside it. There was a small desk on top of which sat a flickering oil lamp and a pot of cold tea. The officer ushered them inside.

"I am only letting you see him because I don't think Mister Prince deserves what is happening to him, understood? And I don't want to annoy your family, they hold the contract to my house. I think there's much more to this case than your folks are telling us Miss Hoddington. If you were seen coming into the station, you are to say you were simply reporting a missing earring, alright?"

"I understand," she muttered. The officer nodded.

"My job is on the line here, just remember that. I know it doesn't mean much to someone as fortunate as you but this is my livelihood and my reputation."

"Officer, I understand, I promise I do."

Annabel thought how laughable it was that he considered her fortunate. If only he knew what her life was really like, the decisions she was going to have to make and the things she had already endured. Patsy was ushered out of the small cell first, as they had previously agreed, leaving Annabel alone.

She paced up and down, rehearsing a speech in her head, wishing she had been granted more time so she could have prepared for this more. The one thing she did not have was time.

Her nails pressed into her sweaty palms in agitation, leaving half-moon shaped indents in the skin. Her stomach twisted angrily, absentmindedly she touched the soft material there, imagining she could feel her unborn child but of course, she couldn't.

"Miss Hoddington, I'll take you through now."

"Thank you, will we be alone? I have something very important to discuss with him."

"Yes Miss, of course. There's nowhere he could go, the corridor is locked."

Her mouth twitched in an attempted grateful smile, following him down the corridor. They stopped three cells before the end and the officer motioned for her to enter.

"I'll be in the office Miss."

Annabel nodded her thanks and turned towards the door as the officer's footsteps retreated down the corridor. She hesitated for a brief second before drawing in a deep breath and walking into the dim space. Her eyes locked on his straight away and her whole body sighed. She clanged the door shut behind her and then Daniel's arms were on her waist, his lips pressing against hers so hard it almost hurt. The second their lips met he trembled with pleasure. Annabel smiled. Clinging to him, all thoughts were instantly wiped from her mind, all worries made insignificant. Everything was complete. When they could no longer go without air they broke apart, their foreheads resting together as their breathing slowed. Annabel's hands went into his hair, her eyes drinking in his face.

"Hello," he laughed.

Annabel ran her hands down to his back and rested her head against his chest, listening to the reassuring sound of his steady heartbeat.

"I thought you'd never come," he whispered, the humour fading.

"Why didn't you reply to my letter?" she whispered back, looking up into his face again.

He blushed slightly, looking ashamed.

"Th-that one?" he pointed towards a small ledge beside his bed, Annabel saw the letter still unopened in its crisp white envelope. "I – I can't read."

His confession was so quiet she almost missed it.

"What? At all?"

He shook his head.

"Oh. I thought you just didn't want to reply."

He looked at her again.

"Why'd I not wanna read it Anna? I'm going to spend the next ten years learnin' to be the best reader in the world so I can take in every word of your letters."

Annabel smiled, kissing him one more time, as hard as she could.

"I love you," she whispered against him, putting all the sincerity she could behind those three little words. His eyes glittered, his mouth turning up into a beautiful smile. "More – more than you'll ever know."

He fiddled with a stray lock of her hair, "I think I do know."

She took a deep breath. She couldn't do this looking into his honest eyes so she looked down at his chest, her voice now shaking, willing herself not to cry.

"We - we can't do this, I can't do this."

Annabel felt his grip tighten on her waist. He tilted her chin up to face him. Try as she might she could not avoid those eyes, showing her just how much she had hurt him with that one utterance.

"I can," he whispered back, determination rich in his voice. "We will find a way – we have to."

"I'm engaged Daniel, I'm getting married. It's already been announced."

All happiness left his face, his expression grew stony.

"I thought – I thought you'd forgotten about him. You told me...so this was all a joke for you?"

He dropped Annabel like she'd burned him. Annabel shook her head.

"No! Daniel it wasn't a joke, I just – I can't explain why but I have to marry him, Daniel I have to."

"You can't explain what? Jus' tell me Annabel! We 'ave to work this out. Is it – is it 'cuz you're back with your rich friends up in that manor and you're ashamed o' me? Do I remind you of bad memories? What is it?"

"You don't – that's not it at all, I love you, I always will, but I have to marry him. I can't turn my back on my family, live alone and outcast for ten years while I wait for you!"

"You think I wanted this? You think this was my plan when I ran away with you?"

"We ran away because Tom was going to kill you-"

"Yes and this turned out so much better than that didn't it? I think I'd rather just be dead than rotting in here alone."

"No, Daniel please don't say that."

She reached for him but he backed away, his jaw tensing in his effort to keep the tears behind his eyes. She was hurting him and it was nearly killing her.

"What's really going on Annabel? There's something you're not telling me." He paused, they both looked at each other in silence.

"Do you love him?" he whispered.

Diamonds Fall

Annabel could see he wasn't going to let her go, the only way to do this in a way that allowed him to move on was to lie to him.

She nodded, Daniel let out an involuntary sob. Her arms ached to fold him into them, her mouth begging her to speak about their child, that it was because of the child she was doing this...she couldn't get rid of any part of Daniel no matter how small, yet she couldn't bear it growing up an outcast which would be the certain future of a bastard.

Her letter to Theodore had been burnt and rewritten seven times in total. As much as she wanted Daniel she just couldn't condemn an innocent baby by making this one selfish choice. Theodore must believe the child was his.

"You're just saying this because – because of your mama, you love me, I know you love me, YOU JUST TOLD ME YOU LOVE ME."

He reached up, grabbing handfuls of his thick blonde hair as his face grew red. When he could no longer bear it he turned his back on her, his shoulders shaking. Annabel, now blinded with tears herself, put her hands on him, pressing her lips into the back of his neck. He spun around, holding her face between his palms as he pushed his lips against hers. He pressed her against the naked stone wall and she let out an involuntary moan. He was like her drug and she didn't want it to end. Would ten years really be all that long to wait? Before she knew it she was kissing him back with the same ferocity, her hands in his hair, his hands still on her face. However, all too soon the reasons she could not be with him came flooding back. With all the will she possessed she broke away and spoke her final four words to the love of her life.

"Goodbye Daniel, I'm sorry."

Before turning her back on happiness forever.

The moment she left the cell her face crumpled. She kept her walk even and her shoulders high, knowing he would watch her go. Daniel called after her desperately but she continued forward without faltering. Once safely outside, she shattered.

Bent double behind a row of dingy looking shops sobs so violently took hold of her that even the horses on the street grew restless. The pain was so severe she thought her heart had been torn clean from her chest, with just the tightened strings of her corset keeping her together.

It was this day, as she lay in a crumpled heap amongst the mud and cobbles, that Annabel's heart broke for the first time, splitting straight down the middle to leave a deep scar forever more.

Chapter Twenty-Four

Annabel tried to appear as normal as possible when she arrived home, still shaken, exactly an hour after she had left, as per instruction. She climbed out of the cab on weak legs, stumbling as her vision clouded once more with the grief of her broken heart. She walked forwards as if on autopilot, keeping her chin towards the sky as if she were simply returning from a shopping trip. Again, as per instruction. Inside however, she was in melt down.

She felt like she had betrayed everyone she had ever cared about; as if she had betrayed herself. The picture of Daniel's face as she told him that final lie, the deep searing pain etched across his features, was burnt into her vision. It invaded her mind every time she so much as blinked, threatening to knock her over completely.

The echo of her shoes on the marble foyer was too loud; the clacking ricocheted against her skull making her wince with every step. When she reached the stairs she clung to the banister with a white knuckled grip to drag along her failing body. Cell by cell she could feel herself slowly shutting down and she knew it was only a matter of minutes before she came apart completely. It was just long enough to get into her chambers and lock the door. She would tell the maids she was to be left alone, that she would not be going down to dinner so she could have one single night to grieve.

When she reached her bedroom she slipped inside as quickly as she could. As she closed the heavily polished door she rested her forehead against the cool surface, closing her eyes in the relief of finally being alone. Tears immediately started to spill over, racing down her cheeks and dripping off of her nose to make dark spots on the carpet beneath her.

"What happened?"

Annabel jumped, her heart racing a thousand miles an hour as the shrill voice of her mother struck up behind her.

"Come on child. Speak."

Annabel swallowed, a sob escaping her lips as she straightened as much as she could, holding her chest as she scrambled to find air amongst her sorrow.

"I told - I told him I couldn't - that - that I couldn't see him anymore."

A new sob racked her body as she heard the words in her own voice, the realisation they were true only adding to her pain. The sob sounded obscene in the now silent room. Looking up at her mother Annabel noticed a tight yet triumphant smile illuminating her face.

"How can you be happy about this? You have brought about the heartbreak of your only child. How can that possibly please you?"

"You are being ridiculous Annabel. I have saved you."

All of Annabel's pent up hatred and anger seemed to come to a head at those words.

She had been saved.

Saved from what?

From happiness?

From fulfilment?

In a fit of red hot rage Annabel swung her hand out towards her mother's cheek. The elder woman was ready. She grabbed her daughter's wrist just before she was struck, digging her nails into the porcelain flesh. Scarlet droplets crawled from the half-moon shaped cuts in Annabel's arms, contrasting ominously with her pale skin. Her mother simply glared.

"I may let you believe this is your show child but it is mine. It has always been mine. You are simply a bit player, a pawn. Don't you ever fool yourself that you can beat me. I always get what I want in the end. One way or another."

Annabel was taken aback by this display of cruelty from a woman she had always considered docile at best. She knew she was a pushy mother but she had always convinced herself Elizabeth had been working towards Annabel's best interests. She saw now how drastically wrong she had been.

Annabel dried her eyes on her free sleeve, straightening up to her full height.

"If this is happening, if I am to marry Theodore, it is to happen soon. We will have the engagement ball this weekend as planned and marry the next. Those are my terms and you will obey them." Annabel tried to keep her voice emotionless and cold but the lump in her throat made it wobble ever so slightly over the word 'marry.' She couldn't imagine herself in a white dress and veil, the image felt wrong, perverted in some way.

"People will talk Annabel." Lady Elizabeth said, her voice as sharp as the edge of a sword and dripping with malice.

"Not as much as I will if you don't follow my terms. I am no pawn mother, I am your child and you've taught me more than you would dare to imagine. Don't give me cause to visit a journalist and accidentally let slip what happened whilst I was away. You see, I always get what I want in the end, one way or another."

Lady Elizabeth let go of her daughter's wrist with deliberate slowness and brushed past her, almost knocking her over with the force of the gesture.

"Write to Theodore. Tell him that you will become his wife next Saturday."

Annabel nodded her head once in acknowledgement of this statement and then she broke. The door slammed shut with an echo of finality and she slid slowly down to the floor.

Annabel imagined Daniel's face every single way she could remember. She pictured every inch of his skin, every freckle, every scar. Her fingers shook with the urge to touch him, whilst the fear of forgetting was almost crippling.

She had figured being alone would be the best thing

for her in that moment but it quickly became unbearable. She needed someone to be with her, someone who understood the position she was in and still accepted her completely. Someone who could somewhat distract her.

Contrary to her own wants Patsy wasn't seen for several hours. She had left straight after she had seen Daniel and taken herself for a walk to clear her mind. Of course, when she too learnt to write, she would continue to be in contact with Daniel throughout his imprisonment. However, her silence nearly drove Annabel mad. It wasn't until late that night, with Annabel's room swathed in velvety darkness, that she appeared at her door and silently climbed into bed beside her.

"I see what you mean now," Patsy whispered after a few minutes. "About abuse happening everywhere. People are just cleverer about it here. They make it seem like your own fault."

Annabel reached out her hand, encasing Patsy's.

"I thought you would hate me for what I did. It was driving me mad."

"Anna I'm the one that told you to do it. I couldn't hate you anyway, I was upset that he was upset but I know why you did it. You're protecting his child, creating a better future for it than the past Daniel and I endured. It's hard but you did the right thing."

Annabel's eyes swam with tears.

"I'm sorry I let him down."

"You did everything you could Anna. You've done so much for us already."

Annabel gave a weak smile.

"He deserves so much more."

"I know," Patsy replied in a matter of fact tone. "And he'll get it...one day."

The two girls lay back and absorbed that information. The thought of Daniel falling in love with someone else was painful for Annabel, so painful she could barely stand it, but she knew it would be the best thing - the only thing - that would set things right between them. She hoped, as she lay there, today was not the last time she would see Daniel. Perhaps their paths would cross again. She dreamed that maybe, one day, he would know about his child. Yet, as soon as the thought had formed, she knew it was impossible.

It would be all out war if they were brought back together again.

It was an ironic twist that, for Annabel, being trapped in that stable was the happiest she had ever been.

Chapter Twenty-Five

Annabel looked down at her gloved hands, clasped demurely in her lap. Just as they were supposed to be.

Tonight was the night of Annabel's engagement ball. In exactly one week's time she would be married to the wealthiest bachelor in England. Everything she had dreamed of a couple of months earlier was on the cusp of coming true and Annabel couldn't be more miserable about it.

Her stomach growled beneath the cinched and beaded plum gown because, despite the elaborate feast, she had managed only a few small mouthfuls of food. She was too nervous - not because she believed people wouldn't like her, everyone liked her - but because she realised she didn't really like herself anymore.

She'd let everyone down.

She'd let him down.

Just the thought of Daniel sent an ice cold stab through her heart. She tried to ignore it, focusing instead on the hundreds of guests twirling in graceful circles beneath her as she sat at the head of the ballroom.

Voices buzzed around her like hungry bees, feeding

on the latest gossip the evening had produced. Luckily no-one had suspected Annabel's shot gun wedding at all. She had scoured the gossip columns on an almost hourly basis for any hint of brewing scandal but there was none. The papers had written about her upcoming wedding as if it were a fairy tale. Everyone put the timing down to her 'ordeal' once they found out she had in fact been engaged for months. It was, to the public, the greatest love story of their generation.

Fake laughter bubbled up and died down almost as soon as it had erupted yet no eyes met Annabel's anymore and, despite the ball being held in Annabel's honour, no voices were directed towards her.

She found herself completely alone in a room full of people.

They glanced at her often of course but never long enough to make eye contact.

The feeling of being watched had never regained its glamour. Now, every pair of eyes was another witness to what could end up as the biggest con of her high society generation. Luckily, everyone deemed her too out of reach, too intimidating to actually meet. The spectators appeared to prefer her at a distance.

Annabel preferred that too.

She glanced away when her mother gestured for Annabel to join her. She looked back down at her gloved hands. She had not spoken to the elder woman since the argument in her room and she planned to keep it that way.

It was when she was on the brink of leaving, debating

whether she could get away unseen by her family - the music was certainly loud enough to drown out the click of her heeled slippers against the marble – when she saw him.

He was the only man she hadn't seen tonight, the only one here she hadn't danced with.

His hazel eyes were taking in her polished appearance as he drew closer, a smile tugging at his lips as the chandelier made his hair glow golden, matching the gleam of his buttons.

"Miss Hoddington," he bowed with laughter in his eyes, taking her gloved hand and touching it against his lips. "You look radiant."

She joined in with his laughter, letting the musical sound of it carry her along further into bliss. As she relaxed back into her chair he placed a tender hand against the layers of silk, beneath which the final piece of Daniel she had left, took shelter inside of her.

"Annabel."

She opened her eyes, startled out of her fantasy and back to the man now standing in front of her. Theodore kissed the ring on her left hand with a gleam of pure joy in his chocolate gaze.

"Would you care for a final dance?"

Acknowledgements

To everyone who has helped me on my *Diamonds* journey, I offer my sincere gratitude.

To Beth Kelly, who was the first person to ever read *Diamonds*. For talking to me about Annabel as if she were a real person and being my first editor, I will be forever grateful.

To Lauren, who was with me when Annabel originally tumbled into my head.

To Molly Phipps, without whom this book would be nothing - my editor, cover designer and best friend, THANK YOU for helping my dream come true.

To my parents for giving me life and love.

And to you, for reading this story, that contains at least half of my soul, I hope you have enjoyed reading it as much as I enjoyed writing it!

Lightning Source UK Ltd.
Milton Keynes UK
UKOW02f1827020615

252781UK00004B/11/P